Love and Cupid and all the sultry things

Love and Cupid and all the sultry things

Love and Cupid and all the sultry things
Kyle Gougeon

Copyright Information
Copyright 2024 Kyle Gougeon

ISBN: 9798327817487

To Tammy, my muse.

Dedicated in loving memory to Dad.

I am a trophy mounted on Cupid's wall, first in line, the famous, though nameless to most. It is neither a gift nor a privilege that I have come to understand the power and the mystery behind his rage. I understand what fuels his lust for tragedy. He knows nothing of love. Cupid was once among the gods. He did not walk alongside them, he never dined with them. He was a mere plaything, a fleeting source of amusement. A jester to poke at their parties. He was fed their scraps, he longed for his revenge. Not against them, but against us. The opportunity presented itself, and he escaped the yard, he snuck through the fences, while they slept. He disappeared into the darkness and we have suffered him ever since.

Cupid is a celebrity and a spectacle. He rules his rowdy place within time and the universe with lies and manipulation. He crushes his will down upon humanity. He wills us to lose, wills us to stumble, wills us to be blind. He has tricked us into believing adoration can be sung through cards and chocolates, adoration lavished through diamonds and roses. I know Cupid, as he knows me. Even as he is praised and celebrated, he can not restrain his cruelty and contempt.

I know the truth. Cupid knows nothing of love. It twists his gnarled mind; his heart has blackened to a charred pearl. He has never felt the avalanche, he has never been lovesoaked. He has never experienced the depths and the lightness, he has never risen through the layers, chewed upon the gristle, love has never

6

ached through his bones. It is the reason he sows jealousy and discontent. He will take the song from a bird, a baby from a mother, he will put the fool into the genius, the devil into a nun. Cupid's frustration speeds his arrows, his frustration gnaws and boils, it wets his horrible fingers and lips. And then he turns it upon us, uses it upon us.

Cupid despises me most; I know this all too well. This intimacy is my reason, my guide, my courage. I hope. He has not destroyed me yet, not in this life. I still wander, I still have my legs, I still wait. Each time I have been born, each life I have lived as my own, there has been the burden of the truth about Cupid. I carry it until it crushes me.

This is an ill-advised tale, at an ill-advised time. I believe I alone can be the narrator in the final chapter of Love and Cupid and all the sultry things.

I do not know when Cupid and I first met. I do not know how and where I may have wronged him. As I look in the mirror today, it is hard to believe I was nothing more than a shiny object which attracted his attention. My memories are pieces of the wreckage he has given me. The glass and the metal and the darkness and the jokes. My memories are scattered across the ages. He gives them to me in my dreams. He gifts them, when they burn like salt, if they stick to me like a scent, follow my steps, moisten the pain. Cupid dresses like a captor and predator, and I like the prey.

It can be humbling; the way time can create truth. Repetition can create truth. When reality is painted and planned and not earned and created.

Cupid is a slayer of kings and a deceiver of queens. Empires have toppled in heaps like matchsticks in his hands. He has crippled lost and forgotten lands and modern civilizations with his kissing plagues. Cowards have been rewarded and brave warriors have fled. Fires have run from the cold, bridges surrender to the waters beneath them, skyscrapers bend at their knees. Presidents have lied and popes have dropped their shorts, lovers have forgotten lovers, and dreams get smashed upon the rocks.

Cupid's misery is his own and it is absolute. It lives in his eyes; it is there in his brutal teeth. It's within the games he plays and the promises he breaks. He offers it like a box of flavored chocolates. He sprinkles his poisons and potions, and he laughs through his madness. His arrows fly and fall swift and sudden, they tear into the very ground.

I will try to maintain there is hope, even when Cupid arrives before the men and women and children can hide. The tiniest hint of light can survive the darkness, touch can conquer callousness. There is hope beyond the noise and the chaos. There is peace beyond the challenge and the silence.

Cupid dances in and out of my memories, he is thick and rude and comes and goes as he pleases. He invades my dreams, I sense where his fingers have been in my sleep soaked mind, in my softened mind. There is an ache behind my eyes, my pulse is heavy in my neck, my ears feel as though they have been kissed. He leaves images, they hang in the day, I cough and spit, they are too much in my mouth.

He wants me to worry beneath the dreams, he wants them pulling, he wants them echoing and taunting. Cupid once laughed and told me we were brothers, he wrapped his arm around my shoulders and told me we were friends and there would never be a secret I could keep from him. He squeezed me tight, and it was all I could do to prevent him from pushing me off the cliff.

======

I was alone last night, there were no memories or dreams. A night that just laid there with no face, silent, an empty space between then and now. A night that wore dark, without fright, without discomfort or rest. Time was neither gained nor lost. My arms and legs had nothing more to do, my eyes fell closed, stunned into sleep. A night as pure as its name, without consequence or reward. Just a blanket I laid beneath.

But I awoke with a thought I hoped Cupid would not hear. I have not seen Her face in so long, I can not see Her face. My hands have a tremor, my lips are dry. I was unaware I have been wanting, wanting for all these years. There is something wrong with the light, and noise is not how it should be. Satisfaction, comfort and anger, numbness, nothing is quite how it should be. There is something wrong with the years. That is another lingering thought. Days have fallen into place, one after another, but there is suddenly something within the years I can not describe.

There is no focus, no context. The world is spinning, I am certain, there is the sun and the moon, the stars, the clouds, I know. There is this single haunting idea growing into a river. I can not explain it to myself. There is something wrong with the scent and the colors. I hoped Cupid would not hear me. There was a tune and a tone, this hanging thought, I could no longer remember Her name. I would be unable to speak Her name aloud in this room.

This lifetime suddenly feels out of place, it has fallen out of step. The others have come and gone, this one seems reluctant to run, reluctant to dance.

Today, this day, seems to have a hole in it. The minutes and hours ebb in and out of it. I walked from window to window, waiting to see if the rain had stopped on the other side of any of them. I can still see my incessant footsteps across the floor. The walls had the feel of a paper bag as the afternoon drew along, they felt like they wanted to give up. I just wanted to find my way out, I just wanted to get out for a while.

The rain has stopped, I am walking a few blocks to a restaurant I know. The streetlights are coming on, I can see them in the puddles beneath my feet. Don't smile at me, I think. I walk, trying to focus upon the feeling I am hungry. I push through the door, it is early enough that there are empty tables and seats. I immediately see Cupid and his party in the corner. There is a proud golden placard on his table, someone has misspelled reserved. There is a plate of pork chop bones on a platter in front of him. There is meat juice on his face. He is getting hungry for hearts. His men call themselves his cousins, they are desperate to sit around him, sit closest to him. Cupid's little blonde bunnies bring him more food and light his cigar. He motions to an empty chair and I reluctantly come over.

He wants to play games tonight, I just want a hamburger. He has a deck of cards. How about deuces, Jack, my boy. Or something simple like go fish. I won't sit with him, I know I am not welcome. I turn to the bar, leaving my back to the room. I can still see his head in the mirror above the taps. Cupid winks at me and holds up a ball of yarn. He wants to play cat with a string, with me tied at the end. He holds up his boxing gloves. I just came to eat, I do not want to take a beating. He puts his fingers into a plate of nachos, I look down into my empty glass and order another.

The chalkboard at the end of the bar says it is Friday night. The place is beginning to fill with people, it is filling like a fishbowl. I glance at the mirror accidentally, Cupid has cheese on his face and a monstrous grin. He slaps a cousin and kisses a bunny, he starts to sharpen an arrow. I'll pay my tab and leave before the arrows begin to fly and land with their sickening thumps.

I walk down the street without the first thought of tonight or tomorrow. I am no longer hungry, but don't feel much more than that. A few more hours and then some version of sleep and then it all begins again. I stop on the bridge for a moment, I realize none of this looks terribly familiar. I linger outside of my thoughts, with my eyes focused upon nothing.

I can not see Her face out there. Why these thoughts are coming to me today, I do not know. I fear Cupid will hear them, yet I can't push them from my mind. There is nothing from the past to suggest there is anything lost, or anything waiting. There is nothing within the lights on the other side of the water. Just unremarkable evenings, unremarkable weeks. I can not taste Her lips.

I have convinced myself I will fall. I will fail. I will not withstand Cupid's will, I haven't the strength to shoulder Cupid's whims. I haven't a reason to resist, I haven't the strength to surrender. I am in between the middle and the unknown, and that is Cupid's favorite place. I'll remember promises never kept and dances never danced, wishes never fulfilled. And he will keep poking his fingers into me. There is a name and a face I feel I have forgotten. Somehow I do not feel proud enough to have a reason. I'll take the long way home, because I feel I am being followed. I sense there is something around the corners, only to find the enormous weight of nothing. I arrive home and it is just as I left it. My tracks have disappeared, my bed remains unmade. My thoughts still hint at betrayal, trying to remember someone I have never known.

======

I wake in the coldest hour with Cupid sitting upon my chest. I can barely breathe, I can not move. His lips are moving but I can not hear him through his overwhelming breath. He taps a knuckle against my forehead. What do you have going on up there, Jack, my boy. He has a woman from the restaurant with him, his arrow is still fresh in her back. He wants to give me another lie and another disappointment, a broken promise and a humiliation. A bitter memory I will have to shake.

I realize I am dreaming, as my arms and legs move through the butter. My own voice is strange to me. Cupid is laughing, your dog don't hunt, Jack, my boy. The woman is laughing and I want to wake up. He says he will tell me what my dreams are and he will let me know when I have them. He spits on my floor and wedges himself through the door. There is a cloudy mocking vision in front of me. I want to kiss Her.

Morning wakes me with her bony hands and a voice like a cigarette smoker. I drink coffee, chewing on the bits of the dream which remain from last night. Cupid's fragments, Cupid's steaming leftovers. He told me he liked it better when I was younger and defiant, he liked it better when I was stubborn and reckless. When I believed in myself, when I believed I could endure. I try to remember those days, how I dressed, how I walked.

There was a pleasure he found in the defiance, a pleasure in the struggle. Cupid wants you to believe you can win, or at least escape. He wants to take your pride, take your freedom, he loves the smokey flavor of it, the feel of it in his hands. I find I have no actual memories of what he says I have given him. I don't remember what he has taken from me. I don't see the faces, I don't feel the kisses or the affections. I can't remember fighting not to be mounted on his wall. I don't remember a time when I did not believe Cupid would always win. He complained if I will not give myself something to lose, he will give it to me. He wants me to ask for pardon, he wants me to ask for pain, he promises me there will be no relief, he promises me there will be no release.

I walk out into the day, heading in no direction, I am trying to feel distraction at my feet. There is no search or reward. There is no panic and there is no purpose. I want to walk like a man with nothing to possess and nothing to lose. I want to walk like a man who has nothing to remember and nothing to forget. Nobody wins, not when you play with Cupid.

Two blocks behind me, a thought fell over me like a spiderweb. I can't hear Her voice.

I come to the water without realizing, another couple of steps and I would have been in it. I find an empty bench and I sit. There is a wedding party moving along the docks, ready to board a vessel for the night of their lives. And there is Cupid, dressed as a preacher, collecting everyone's tickets, smirking through his smile.

The bride looks lovestruck, her dress flows like

happiness. The groom looks terrified, and the guests are a little drunk and a little sad. I can see the contempt for the human heart spread thick across Cupid's face. He would rather feed them to the sharks than sink the ship, I can see it in his beady eyes.

The bride is beautiful. This night seems to be coming in a hurry, dressed in silver, it seems to be dressed more for me. I breathe easy, as I sit here. I am curious as to why I smile to myself, at myself, as though I am looking down upon myself. I am up to no mischief, I wish no one anything, especially harm. I feel a warm storm coming across my chest and across my lips. There is a soul whispering to me, and she is lovely, though I find no reason or name or face or fire to match with her. There is something in the wind, something in the distance. She is pulling herself with wings, she is drawing closer.

I shake my head and rise to my feet, I do not know this feeling, I do not know if it is a reason to believe.

I drink tonight, not from misery, not to forget. I drink in the silence the radio and television can not provide distraction from. I can barely form the question in my own mind tonight. What if you can leap from Cupid's basket. The solitude within these pressing walls gives no pain, and no relief. I can't see Her face out there, I can't hear Her voice. I feel I am wearing another man's clothing, living another man's life. Struggling to find another man's memories. These pants don't fit quite right anymore, perhaps these thoughts are no more mine than these boots that pace corner to corner, line to line, inch by inch, minute by soaking minute.

These regrets may not even belong to me, these shortcomings, these failures. This emptiness is not my birthright, this weight is not my burden. The day began with its sun, I never

14

asked these questions before. These ghosts do not haunt me. Cupid was wrong, I have nothing to offer, nothing to sacrifice, not even the losing hand. I have assumed the sentence of another man, and that is why there is no tearful, joyful remorse.

I have nothing to feed Cupid. I have no way to quench his thirst, to satisfy his lust. There are no photographs, no maps, no letters. There are no feelings of longing, there is no desperation for the past or second chances. If these steps were mine, if this journey were mine, I would see the path. I would feel the path. There is no loneliness, no loss, no apologies to whisper, no wrongs to right. There is no distinction between yesterday and today but what they are named. I have the same face in the mirror, with the same eyes. I am not troubled, I am not indifferent. There is no deception, no honesty, no trickery or treachery, no exaggeration, no forgetfulness.

Cupid wants most what exists in the heart. What tries desperately to exist in the heart, before he can get his hands on it. I have no scars and no joys, I have nothing with weight. I have no soulful memories, no intimate memories, I have no meat for him, except for my dreams. I am a forgotten man with nothing to forget. Nothing to rediscover, nothing to yearn. Just the slow ache of time and Her face I am suddenly trying to remember. Cupid desires most what keeps the dark at bay, he wants what holds the door and holds back the fear. He wants the safety and the comfort and the dreams. I can not find them, not in the cupboards, not in my pockets, not hidden secretly in a box. It is what I have never read about, never enjoyed, never played a song about.

I can not walk on these legs anymore, I can not sit on this chair. Where is this voice and where is this pretty face. I know nothing of fairytales, nothing of love and loss, passion and grief. I am beginning to doubt my own mind. Build the walls to be torn down, burn the secrets to keep them quiet. The drums of time, the passing of the years, that is what I have known. There are no palaces, no magical gardens, no tearful promises. There are no mysteries to the night, no clenching hands. There are no thorns, no thrones, no thrown oaths, no depths to the colors, no weepy eyes. There is no pursuit of the truth, no pursuit of the past. There is the cold steady wash of the years over the rocks. And Cupid playing his fiddle, and eating from my plate, emptying my plate.

Suddenly I am crushed by the sense of waiting, waiting with no urgency, without purpose. Waiting for an end, or a beginning. For Cupid's arrow to fly or his guillotine blade to drop. Waiting for his sense of humor to fade, for his patience to fade, for his amusement to grow stale. Waiting for a fist to the nose, a scream in the night. I find myself standing still, a man who does not know where he has been, a man without direction. A man with no meat on his bones, without the spirit to surrender or roll over or stay still. Trapped in a photograph of a life I haven't lived, and I can almost hear Her asking where I have been.

======

I wake somehow knowing I don't want to have another man's feelings again. I don't want to spend another night in another man's life. I gather my legs beneath me and walk with a purpose for the first time since I can remember. I devour bacon and eggs, hashbrowns and toast, I finish a third cup of coffee and ask for a fourth. I can not see Her face, but I pay my bill and walk back to Cupid's raucous table. I push his boxing gloves onto the floor, and nod to the door that leads to the alley. And there, between the dumpsters, in the warm sunshine, I take the beating of my life. I feel like I want to laugh and sing. Cupid is standing over me, removing his gloves, I can barely see him through my swollen face. He says I look like someone who thinks he has meat on his bones. See you soon, Jack, my boy. I try not to fall asleep with my mouth on the pavement. I try to believe.

I am snatched back into consciousness with a jerk, back into the world, sitting on a hard chair. The daylight is pressing through the curtains. I haven't a scratch on me, haven't a bruise, not a single calling card from Cupid's blows. My legs have no memory of how I came to return home. There is a faded photograph laying upon my chest, I have studied it with my eyes, without picking it up. The edges are worn as though it were held too long, too many times, too desperately. The picture has faded beyond recognition.

Cupid wants me to have a memory, he needs me to have a memory. Something to hold, something to lose. My head is thick with silence, I hear nothing but my own heartbeat. I dreamed of the endless days of a past life, long days of torment in Cupid's dungeon. The walls were made of cold cruel rocks, they were rounded by time, rounded by incessant trickling waters. The damp air ate at my lungs, the chill saturated the ragged clothing I wore. I listened to the water, day and night, unable to sleep. The light was a hanging listless gray. There was no difference between day and night. Not to me. It was impossible to know how long I had been there, or for what reason. I was certain I was not born there, but I would surely die in this room. The weight of silence overcame the pain of hunger, it slowed the sinking madness. I had long since given up screaming, calling for help. I had thrown my voice against the walls, up towards the ceiling I could not see. The only response was a mocking echo. And then the occasional low chuckle, beyond the door.

No one could hear me, no one could see me. I dreamed I could not remember, finally, when I had last spoken aloud. My hands gave up pounding against the door. I no longer had the will to cross the room and peer under the door. I would stare at what slid beneath it and into my room. A crusted bread, a shallow pan of cold broth. I don't know how long it would take me to rise and then crawl, to desperately devour the food. I knew one day I would no longer have the strength to endure Cupid's compassion.

He was my gaurd, my warden. He was my burden. He had been my judge and my jury. If I was quiet for too long, he would bring spiders, and rats, he would shove them beneath the door. He did not want my surrender. I would plead through the heavy, heavy door, and receive only silence. I dreamed the massive door opened. I did not know how long it had been since I had moved or eaten or opened my eyes. I could not say if I had slept or died. I sat in the farthest corner of his dungeon. The walls had long since stopped playing their tricks, stopped rolling and walking close, laughing and falling. They were endless and impassable, perhaps bored with me. Cupid walked heavily across the dirt floor. He kicked aside his rats, stepped upon his own spiders.

I waited, expecting the end, the glorious end, the delicious end. I exhaled, and welcomed the strike, the final blow.

He looked upon me with contempt and disgust. He raised my eyes with his horrible sticky fingers beneath my chin. He showed me a small window, it was an impossible window in an impossible wall. From the corner, from my lowest point, at my weakest, I could see out the window. I knew in my dream there would be no end. There would be no compassion. I knew it as true as the lies which rattled around in my head, the lies I told myself to prevent the last of my mind from vanishing. My strength would leave me first, then my hope, then my sanity. No, Jack, my boy, your hope is what I will take last.

I found the strength to reach the wall, made it to a knee, and briefly stood. The window was just beyond reach. The walls could not be climbed, even if I had not been broken, they could not and would not be climbed. I surrendered to the corner, laid there, brushing the spiders from my legs. I laid until I was finally still and saw no more. There was nothing in the blackness but Cupid whispering inaudibly, once again from beyond my heavy door.

I dreamed my eyes opened. There was a light, a remembered light, it was stunning and painful. It was mine and just for me. I slowly focused and saw through it. Through the window I saw a tree, an enormous willow, and beneath a bench made for two. Soon a figure appeared, silently, softly, a silhouette, a beautiful young woman. I could not see her, yet I could, I was convinced, she held flowers in her hands. She dropped them, slowly, one after another, as the light steadily diminished. She rose when the last struck the ground. And she left.

My eyes opened for the light, once again, time and again, for what I could only assume was day after day, maybe week after week. I would see the enormous willow, and the quaint bench for two. She would appear, I would shout, trying to gain her attention, searching with my hands and waving arms for her eyes. I screamed, hoping to see her face. Trying to drown out the madness and the unintelligible whispering of Cupid from just beyond the door. Each time, she faded with the light.

I regained my strength through the suffering. I paced the floors of the dungeon, I pounded upon the walls. I paced off the hours of the morning, each one, I dreaded the afternoons. Crying out, I was crying out. I strained and stared at the flowers and watched them drop, one by one, I watched her feet press the grass flat, until everything disappeared into the inevitable, the darkness. And Cupid whispered, insufferably, he whispered wet beyond the door, it pooled around my feet, the whispers froze me in the night. I could not shout to drown him out, no noise, no words, passed my dried lips. He made the nights longer than the days. He would tell me I promised to meet her there, I had pledged my life and love to her. A life of devotion. She was faithful, so patient, so earnest and trusting. She returned each day to wait, scarcely looking up from the flowers in her hands, waiting with a timeless faith, waiting with a timeless strength. Waiting until the light of another day faded away, wondering why I would not come, as I promised.

I had pledged her a lifetime, I dreamed I watched her disappear. Slowly. I suffered each day, I died a little more each day, watching her beauty wilt with my broken promise, watching in silence as her spirit wilted just like the flowers she dropped one by one. Until she stopped coming to sit beneath the bench made for two, beneath the willow.

I cursed Cupid, his laugh echoed beyond the door. He grew fat, I grew weaker, he grew hungrier and I abandoned my will and my fight in the darkest corner. His laborous torture, his triumphant moment. A promise never to be, a love never to be lived. A face unseen, disappearing into the darkness, lost forever to the past.

I dreamed as a broken man, and awoke, feeling its weight slide from my shoulders and down my back. I stared at the dirt from the dungeon on the sheets at the foot of my bed.

======

There is not a room in the world Cupid can not find and violate. There is not a feeling or celebration or a breath of forgiveness he does not want his fingers on. He would have us all behind the fences, he would have us all in chains. He has been granted too much freedom. He has trampled through the chaos of centuries. He knows the truths before we can learn them and has already seasoned them with his lies.

I am following or chasing my own footsteps down the sidewalk, I have no particular place to be. I have this gnawing feeling I am running late. I enter a place and the room is filled with people who look like cardboard cutouts, their drinks are wet and their conversations are dry. Cupid is at a table in the corner, a massive table. He has marinara sauce all over his shirt and a hungry look around his eyes and mouth. He makes no move or gesture towards me, he has a cigar small in his fat filthy hand. He is surveying the room, he must smell blood in the water. Someone gets up from his table and nudges me as they pass. I look down at my hands and order my food. I smile at them and show them all my teeth. Yes, Cupid dances really well with his knuckles, but I am here and about to eat, and it appears he has no interest in me tonight.

I am halfway through the better part of a ten dollar steak. Cupid rises from his chair and waves his finger in the air and everyone cheers and laughs and the band begins to play. He spreads his poison and everyone delights. I stand with a little dignity, stand while I still have the chance to walk. People are dropping to their knees not to duck or evade but to be purposefully struck. I move like a nameless shadow.

Six steps on my way and I feel there is something in this city, there is something in the distance, there is something in this night. My legs can't seem to find their path, and my mind and memory can not help. The streets are twisting over themselves. The lights are turning themselves back inside. The night drops around me, as though trying to pull me to the ground. A face flashes, Her face, as real as heat in my eyes, heat across my lips. I pause for a moment, thinking there is no way home. The clocks drop their tired hands, all the children stop playing, no one will quiet the dogs barking in the distance. Cupid gave me a nightmare I have nearly forgotten. The closer to the edge we travel, the harder we try not to fail. I wander closer to the sweetness of the darkness, inching towards its center. I thought I saw a face. I am suddenly without fear, I am obstinate, blind and deaf, I feel reckless and heavy footed. I wonder if Cupid can hear me now.

His parade is approaching around the corner, it is obnoxious and loud and bright. He is standing through the sunroof of a limousine, raising and waiving his hands like a shepherd over his flock. Men and women are squealing and shrieking, laughing and dancing. The arrows will soon fly, everyone last one of them will be struck, tagged and numbered.

The morning will sort out the winners and the losers, those with regrets and those with and without memories.

I turn where the sidewalk bends, to avoid the hysteria and confusion. I don't seem to know this path or this street, it is impossibly unfamiliar. I walk a little farther, feeling like a man with an unremarkable past, no foreseeable future. I have done nothing and gained nothing and lost nothing. I have occupied a space in this world, nothing more, nothing less. Just Cupid's parlor games. I am curious, I have never been here, I have no memory of this street. The parade presses behind me, growing closer, I will press on towards the darkness, it looks like it is raining ahead. My steps continue and a purple glow is wrapping itself through and within, beginning to swirl. A purple becoming deep shades of cascading blue. I stop, allowing my eyes to focus. It is there, just ahead, in the sudden silence, in a warming quiet and calm.

A lost memory from Cupid's dungeon flashes in my eyes. A face in the window, a breath in the room. It said I will see you in the next life. I will feel you. I will find you.

In triumphant surrender, my steps take me farther. I am a man with nothing to offer Cupid, I am meat for him to poke. I have nothing to lose in his games. I hold my face up to the rain, I raise my face and keep it there. I am suddenly above the known and the familiar, I am above the convenient and the rot. I am beyond the known, beyond the terror. I am in the peace, a new peace. I am untouched and unheard. I am out of the reach of yesterday and today, I am free from the wheels of the world, I am free from any dream, free from any tomorrow.

I am in a cloud, I am in a wisp of air, I am in a memory of no one, but something holds me. There is soothing familiarity, a discovery and newness, a rebirth. There is power without control, a force without selfishness. The lightning is draping me in lines of deepening blue. There is a burst of truth with heat, heat with no anger, heat with no punishment. I float and the storm wraps around me painlessly, high above the sleeping eyes of the world. She is gently pushing, willing me to wake, touching my forehead, telling me I don't have to remember. She runs her hands through my hair and I am in disbelief. We embrace, She is the light, She is my force of nature.

I know you.

I hear a whisper. You are my favorite.

We embrace in long lost and new silken movements. We are unseen by the day, we are hidden from the night. The angels conceal their joy behind their hands when they laugh. I will be struck by the magic they invented for us. I will keep the promises in this hand and the other. I am in your storm and there is no other place I need. The cannons of time have stilled. The rivers of want lick their lips and stare at us. My heart is in your hands, and my soul is being cradled.

She is Love, and I am her Leo, and Cupid despises us most.

My eyes open, before I am fully awake, I wonder if it was all a dream. The ceiling hangs above me, looking mostly innocent. I can not remember my steps home from last night. My clothes are on the floor, my wallet, my belt, my shoes. It looks like a massacre. But no memory. I lay still with a sudden tiredness. I can't remember what I needed to do today. I lay in this stale purposeless bed, the walls are in their places in this purposeless room. Everything seems normal and innocent enough. If it were all just a dream, I would accept it. I would want another.

I rise slowly, like a man overcome, like a man nuisanced by the new day. I wish to be back in the light, I wish to hear that whisper again. If last night was real, perhaps I am afraid to know the truth. I should hide it in the cupboards, hide it behind the walls, beneath the rugs, I should hide it safely away in the silence and the darkness. I can not tell if it is relief or fear which holds my hands steady. I can not decide if one dream should be so important.

My love, my Leo, everything will be fine.

Yet I know Cupid will stop at nothing to keep us apart. He will exhaust every trick, every cruelty, every coldness. He will utilize every hardship, every distraction. He has shown me dreams, as well, he has come to me in dreams. I have choked and suffocated for a lifetime, my soul has not longed or searched or soared in what must be forty years. How many ways can I say it? There is danger in my heart, a fear of loss before I even possess anything. There is true raw excitement in my blood, a fever in my bones. I have already lost hours of the day, I feel a blend of curiosity and dismay. If Love was real, she must be kept a secret, if Love was a dream, she must be even more secret. Cupid will have his sick pleasure in my loss, whether it is real or not. I stare long into the mirror, wanting to know if I can wear the look of a broken man, a defeated, stoic, stupid man, wanting to see if there is still a wince about my eyes, as though I am expecting his next blow.

And where shall I find you again? I feel hope, and that is dangerous. There is hope beyond my stare, there is green beyond the blue of my eyes. If you are real, I don't want to betray us. If you are real, I want you to take me where he can never find us. If you were but a dream, I want you to swallow me, and lose me in the night. And keep me. You are a whisper in the room. I know you, Leo, I have found you.

I walk out into the world, I walk the tightrope of a love eternal. I walk like a man with meat on his bones. I walk with the freedom of a man bound in Cupid's chains, I walk with the freedom of having one hand freed. I walk with the freedom to dream and love, to live and love, I walk with desire. I walk too noisily, my steps clanging down the sidewalk. I walk with fear and secrecy. This may well be a poorly timed walk in an ill-timed life. The day hasn't decided to make way for the night just yet, they are showing each other their claws, the world bleeds between the sun and the moon. Everything is curious and waiting. The streets are mysteriously empty, with just us strays about. I wonder if everyone is just waiting, or working, or wanting to see if there is a change in the air. A gentle movement from silence to peace. Something to change the dismal to the unknown, something to give us a chance.

There seems to be no one here to take a stand for humanity. There is no one will to battle Cupid, the monster. The warriors are gone, the beast slayers, the wizards and the wisemen. The defenders of truth and light, of men and women, of souls, they are all gone, or in hiding, or retired sitting in rocking chairs on their porches, afraid of their own shadows, afraid of Cupid's shadow. Where are the soldiers? All that remain are the broken, the blind and the deaf. Cupid is the villain playing the role of the hero. We all gather for the scraps from his table. I can't remember the last time I saw my own courage.

What of the gods who created him and allowed him to go free? They sleep in their luxury, they sleep lost in history, lost in their wine and their own stories. We suffer his wars and accept his truces. We accept he ruins the day and wreaks havoc upon the night. We are numb, walking across our own bleeding hearts on the floor. And there is the guilt, the powerlessness I feel. I am the one he despises most, and my own actions and reactions are slow and brittle at best.

With all this mystery and madness in the world, I enter a place with an all you can eat buffet. I feel the need to be anchored and heavy, slowed and subdued. The windows are steamed tight and shut. I accept my empty plate, and see Cupid and his entourage have the right side of the restaurant filled and loud. There will be no silent remorseful overeating here tonight. I scan the dishes and offerings, losing my appetite, wondering which pans he has stuffed his horrible fingers into, wondering where he has breathed, wondering where he has sweated.

I take a table farthest from the crowd. There is a lover's lane, gathering over there, a murmured blur of sound and dishes and dresses and sweaty hands. Lambs gathered for the slaughter. I try to bury myself in my plate, first in the chicken, then the potatoes. I feel Cupid's heavy stare upon me, he is motioning me over. I reluctantly rise, my legs feel as though they may betray me. Cupid stabs his fork down onto his plate, it strikes, it sparks, loud and angry and greedy. Stabs his fork into the romance, stabs his fork into the sentiments and the longings and the promises. He devours them all, raw, he devours them hungrily, their juices spill onto his shirt, they dance a moment until they are soaked in and die. His hands are wet, his forearms glisten, he motions me closer. His chin is dripping, it all rolls down into his neck.

There is something wrong with your face tonight, Jack, my boy. Cupid frowns at me over a biscuit, he bites into it and stuffs it into his mouth. I do my best to act quiet and beaten. He goes back to playing roulette with Justice and Destiny. He has most of the chips, they are looking humbled, they are losing badly. He laughs loudly. If they want to change their luck they should play me. I nod to them, they are essentially strangers, I almost feel sorry for them, but they are the ones who chose to sit at his table, whether by choice or chance or misfortune. They could have sat with me. I sense they do not want to be here anymore than I do. Cupid stares long and hard into my face, I try to hide all of my hope behind my teeth. Before he can speak, he is brought a cake and a king's dish.

And suddenly the jukebox plays in the corner, someone, somewhere, has found themselves enamored enough, or interested enough, to want to dance. I stand and walk away unsteadily and unnoticed. The tables break up into groups, the groups into pairs. Cupid loses his smile and drops his biscuit and his eyes nearly close. The games are forgotten, the debts are forgotten, I am forgotten. The three of us, Justice and Destiny and I, pay our bills and exit separately, with the skin still on our backs.

I take a long rambling route home, the moon is light on my shoulders, I can nearly taste the night between the buildings, between the streets and the sky. There is something waiting. Something larger than me. I stop to cough, as if I were indeed holding a secret, keeping it hidden deep inside.

I believe I have breathed this air before, not in this life, possibly in a dream. My chest is clenching itself around my hidden secret. It is growing there, it will be loosed soon enough. It won't matter to Cupid if Love is real or dreamed. I am standing in front of the old familiar building, debating if I remember how to get in. How many years I have been here, I scarcely remember. Last night seems to occupy my memories. I will go inside, if it keeps me safe and quiet tonight. Tomorrow will come with answers, I hope, that is where they exist. Just there, just within reach. I enter my room and turn on a single light, sit in a chair. And wait, heavy in the present, heavier in mood. The clock on the table has stopped, it has dropped its hands and stopped. The familiar feelings of hunger and anger are trying to return, but I feel a memory twisting herself around me. I need your light, my Love, I need your light, if you are there.

=====

I dream of the illusion of Time, the elusiveness of Time, in her flowing robes and evening gowns. Time, with her steady unrivaled certainty in her voice. Revered, her name spoken for ages and never forgotten. Her delicate invasiveness, her deliberate erosion. Time lives on a mountain of her own, created by her own hands. No one dares intrude, no one trespasses or attempts to contradict her. She is majestic and respected and feared. She allows the world to spin across her fingertips, her judgements are final, her reach is endless.

No one will ever escape the hands of time. She was born an innocent idea, she has grown to an element of the universe. She can manifest joy and tragedy, panic and delight. At her worst, at her most cruel, she can bring doubt and annihilation, her movements can be terrible and swift and unpredictable. But she can be gentle, she can blow like the breeze, she can be slow and beautiful, thick as honey, unending, forgiving, lavishing us with evolution, rewarding us with just a little more.

I dream I am silently watching her as she moves through a field of tall grass. She walks in an effortless, tireless way. She has never known a weight or burden, she has never known loss. Time can offer and steal away, she does not suffer, she does not notice changes in the universe, when they are ours, when they are hers. She knows nothing of dangers or challenges. Time is both real and imagined, she is unconquerable and insufferable. She lives regally and comfortably in all the worlds we create. She is not influenced by the senses, she knows nothing of the trappings of any existence. Time is not confined to a box or a watch or a clock. She is chased, she is pursued, she is lost and gained. She calmly observes the circumstances she creates.

I dream and watch, respectfully, from a great distance, knowing she is aware of me, knowing her presence is everywhere. She is unmoved, she is not threatened. I can offer no resistance, I can do her no harm. I can only assume she has grown accustomed to being watched. From her mountaintop, Time can observe the world she influences. The sun as it sets, the moon as it rises, the oceans as they endlessly flow to the shore. She keeps her back to that which she has forgotten. The rest remains in her hands. The past in her right, the future in her left, the present hovering somewhere near her lips.

I dream, stunned by her beauty, fearful of her power. She walks a lazy trail down bedside a tree line. She stops, because there is a young girl there. From my view she seems to be speaking from kindness. She moves the girl's long blonde hair from her face and holds her chin. I can not tell if she is singing or whispering, but they are smiling. She gives the girl something, something I can not see. Time and the little girl nod and part ways as quickly as they encountered each other. I watch as Time continues her effortless walk, and never once looks back.

The girl has vanished and Time proceeds, and I can feel the years pressing into my face, deeper than the growing lines and whiskers, I feel them upon my eyes and my lips. I dream I want to wake, and I don't know how and I don't know when and I don't know for how long.

=====

My eyes open and chase my surroundings. The walls are waiting for me, the morning outside, too, it is waiting for me. There are new shadows in the room, my imagination tells me there are footsteps on the other side of the door. I must still be dreaming, though no one is laughing and no one is singing. I admit to myself I am fully awake.

I can feel the movements where the other pillow would be. Were I not alone and not so familiar with being alone. I feel a warm hand touch my stomach, rise to my chest. There is a breath at the side of my neck. There is a sweetness and a whisper. My Leo, my sweet sweet Leo. I had to find your soul to find your face. A weightless wing drapes across my shoulders, I feel like I am home, my lips find a kiss and search for another.

My soul has no questions, my heart has no fear. I hear my own voice say good morning, Love. We lay in a tender quiet world, there is nothing to reach us, nothing to steal us. My eyes are rich and wet with disbelief. She silently, carefully, soothes these bones, there is light in her hair, love in her eyes. We move slowly, only to remember the touch of another place at another time, we kiss to remember another kiss. A love exquisite, a love freed. We share a smile only the two of us will ever know. You are my favorite.

All I know is you are here and you will never leave. There is no movement, no feel, beyond this, beyond us. Let the world and life fall from buckets, we know nothing but this soft moment, nothing beyond this long slow embrace. We can't hear the machines and the drums and the hammering and the demands. The morning has us close at her chest, she is breathing on us. Stay here. Life grinds away out there, outside, somewhere, not here, not in our sighs, not in our swollen touches, not in our ravenous kisses. There are but the thunderous moments, when they exhale, and we hang tightly together. There is the delicious urge and want, I have my Love in my arms, and there is nothing else.

Heaven can keep its sickly hands in its pockets, hell can keep its torments and temptations. I am bathing in lovewhispers and I will accept them over any truth or hope. Let the angels and the devils have themselves, let the world run, let yesterday ambush today and today ambush tomorrow. I have a taste of happiness, I have a safer place within these arms. I have eyes opened which will never be closed. Two hearts have tasted and will never be filled. Love has spilled across me, I am ruined to the world, and it is fantastic. I will never take a breath or a step in the same way. I tell her with my blood and bones, my heart and soul. Love whispers into my ear. My Leo, I know.

Not all promises are smashed upon the rocks, not all promises are spoken by liars. Some are spoken by lovers. What has been endured and learned can be released. Love kisses my cheek, and the mud and the muck have released my feet. She kisses my cheek and I ask her if she will show me how she spreads the stars and the moon, and she smiles, and says if I promise, she will.

I promise.

======

I have faith with Love upon my lips and a promise to see

me tonight. I walk out into the daylight and face the harsh reality. There are no secrets kept from Cupid, they are his to discover, his to steal, his to trample and throw into the trash with all the broken promises. I know from my dreams, he will take me from her. I have two choices, and I feel my own legs beneath me. I can face him or run, and since my courage escaped me years ago, I don't know why and I can't remember when, I am not certain I can face either choice.

Love has a freedom and a strength all her own. Cupid is the keeper of pains of the past. I sense they are two forces about to collide. There is an immense stone wall in front of me, it curls around me, it sits like a waiting smile. There is a darkness only Cupid possesses, he wields it in his hands and curses and arrows. I am fresh from Love's arms, I wonder if the daylight is deceiving me. Love arrived and I feel her heat in my hands at this very moment. And I can still sense the cold stare of Cupid's contempt. I can smell his awful breath behind his menace and words. I have no courage to lose, I have nothing to surrender, nothing to reveal, nothing but my divine meeting with Love. Her sweetness, her promises spilled through heavy lips, and her light. I chew into the concrete sidewalk. I am half the man I was never meant to be. I will love Her, more than I could in a thousand dreams. I feel as though I am beginning to walk like a man who thinks he has meat on his bones.

I promise, I promise under my breath, in the safety within the pause between breaths. Somewhere in the living void between my mind and heart and soul. There must be safe shadows and silence. I make promises for only her to hear. Thoughts can be dangerous, hope even more so, Cupid can smell them, sense them, devour them ravenously. I promise we will be together to the end, this time. I will not surrender, I will not be made to disappear. A life we have never known. A rescue from the heartbreak, from the pain and turmoil and doubt. A love uninterrupted.

Here I am, in this world's light, and the rage of Cupid

seems to stand before my every step. It is a mystery I have yet to solve, a wall impossible to scale or breach. I tell myself it is not the length or the words of the promise, it is the truth and fire behind it, it is the breadth and width, its muscle and veracity. I push the door open. Cupid's mood is heavy and apparent tonight, I can see it in the way he stabs into his meatloaf. I must keep appearances, I seek no eye contact. There will be some mischief and misery tonight, the room slowly bubbles and begins to fill. I want to maintain my secret love. There will be a boiling party tonight, there will be pain tonight. He is angrily pressing his fingertips into the tablecloth, spreading the mashed potatoes like a frustrated child. It is going to come quickly tonight, I try to lower my head into my shoulders a bit more, no one in the room knows what is coming.

I am here only to maintain appearances, to show Cupid his fist is still at my jaw, his knuckles are in my sleeping brain. I am here, ordering the taco special. I feel his eyes running up and down my back. He finally motions for me to come over, I try to walk as though I am defeated. I don't like your face tonight, Jack, my boy, it's not sitting right on your head. He wants me to know he can squash me like a fly on his table. I try to keep Love out of my mind and out of my eyes. He asks if I remember the old days, the good old days, when dogs were not allowed out of their yards. I slump a little, trying to appear more broken.

The time comes for Cupid's game, for his favorite parlor trick. I've witnessed it countless times, and if I am not going to play, I am going to watch. He wills it. He devours the air in the room, creates a vacuum for his own amusement. First, he removes hesitation, and then modesty. The players change but the dance is repetitive. It may be the doctor who finds the cozy corner with the barmaid. The teacher moves past the lawyer and takes the hand of the bus driver. The weatherman sees his chance to console the lawyer and she says yes, the folksinger embraces the preacher, and so it advances like slow torture, these strangers from just hours before.

Cupid directs and harasses, pokes and provokes, his fingers working like those of a conductor. He hasn't the ability to manipulate time, but the vacuum is an hourglass, he shakes it and watches the pieces scatter and resettle, mingle and begin again. Some will find misery in the morning, some will wake with sticky memory, some will recall nothing at all. Cupid will order more meat and wait for the rest to return.

I've witnessed his hysteria and seen the sick pleasure he takes in it. He adds suffering to the insufferable. He will forget their names and faces, for they mean nothing to him. But I will not be forgotten, it seems, I will never be set free. Whether it is through strength or luck or will, I rise from my chair. I want to leave, go outside, I want to let my thoughts drift back to Her. I allow my thoughts to drift back to you. Cupid does not object, he gives me his eyes, and I fear I have been careless. Now his men, his cousins, stand one by one, intending to follow me out the door.

I purposely take a long, meandering path home. I stop and look at magazines, I buy one, and a pack of cigarettes. The cousins are behind me on both sides of the street, there must be six or seven of them. They follow me noisily, like hyenas, they want me to know they are there. They are all just sacks of meat, eating the droppings from Cupid's table, they jump when he snaps his fingers, they wash his cars, mow his lawn, feed his dogs. I pause beneath a streetlight, hoping there will not be any trouble, hoping someone will see and intervene. But I haven't seen a soul for blocks. Boys, I say, Cupid could have just asked me, or talked to me. Or beat my brains out. There is one with a mustache, he is the only one I have ever heard speak. He says Boss is busy. I noticed, yes, I noticed, Cupid is going to have his love massacre tonight, his love tragedy, with every poor lonely soul in that place. There was blood in the air tonight, it was going to be a messy meat grinder.

They are intent on coming with me. I hope Love is patient. I hope Love is not there, or at least hiding. I hope.

I pause my own treacherous thoughts. Mustache says Boss didn't like my face tonight. I have betrayed myself. We reach my front door, I pretend to have difficulty with my keys, I make noises, I am coughing. Oh, don't be in there. I enter first, and Love's footprints and shadows are everywhere I look. I feel her thick in the room, I breathe her in the air, the place is saturated, colored by her. They push me inside and push me aside, I want to cry out. They check the corners and all the closets. Mustache is telling Cupid they can't find nothing I could be hiding, and yes, they checked the bed, they looked under the bed. They haven't opened that door. I take a deep breath, wondering if I can handle six meatsacks. Mustache shoves me against the wall and spits on the floor, and they all exit.

I close the door with a hard slam, I lock it and relock it. I feel Love, heavy and sensual in the place. The walls and windows are giggling, the floor clears its throat. My Leo, what kept you, she asks, coming from the bedroom.
I sigh and rub my hands across my face. Cupid. Cupid kept me. I tell her of every dream and memory I have, everything I have ever suffered, everything we have ever suffered. He is the one who can ruin me, he is the one who can ruin us. I feel as though I am explaining the trials and lives of another man. Love tells me she has no idea who Cupid is. She tells me her soul has found mine. Nothing from the darkness, nothing from truth or fiction, nothing from the past or nightmares will separate us. Cupid despises me most, and she does not believe in him.

Love does not believe Cupid can strangle the light or soften the passion. There is nothing in the darkness, there is nothing that is coming to harm us. I shiver like a man and Love takes my hand. It brings me comfort Love has never known Cupid. Not like I have, not in the least. She sits beside me and fills the room, there is no boogeyman. She has occupied the room, she stops the minutes and the hours and takes a breath. We are but a kiss away, a heartbeat away. This feels like purity and innocence, like comfort, after a lifetime of battles. I am not denied, I am not deceived. There is a lightness, a certainty, a magnetism. She places one foot over the other, she rests her head softly against my shoulder.

I promise I will love you carefully, I will love you slow and deep and rhythmic. I will love you like an animal. I will love your heart, I will love you as were intended to be loved, as you were born to be loved. With gratitude and graciousness, humbly, without fear over envy. I will love you leading you up the stairs, chasing you up the stairs. I will love you as the words drip from the page, as all words drip from my memory, as the years fade and the days grow and I learn to speak again. I will love you as one who can never be lost or stolen, as one who comes to me with a whisper and a fever and a hope, and I will offer everything, everything that I am, everything I could ever become. Just to be the happiest man alive, the happiest man who has ever lived. I will love as though I am drinking the sun and bathing in the moonlight, without privilege or pride or prejudice. I will love you until the towers fall and the ground pulls back its teeth. I will love you in a dress or boots or jacket or wings. I will love you in the wind, I will keep away the rain and the cold. I promise. As history pulls its blanket to its neck, as memory leaves us like an evening fire, we will possess, we will have ourselves, we will have our secrets and our pleasures. Should the birds lose their songs and forget their way, should stars become unloved and forget how to play. I will love you still. I will love you more. I will love you in the madness, I will love you in the quiet. When my legs fall from beneath me and my hands can no longer carry the truth or the fascination. I have waited through memories and lifetimes, for a moment, for a passing of seconds. And here are your eyes. I promise. I promise. I look upon your face, I look into your face, and I see how you stare right through into my soul. We are not the weak, we are not the meek or timid. We have no sins. We have waited years and ages, our fresh souls will not be denied. Our freed souls will not be denied. With trust and might, with my hand in yours and your hand in mine, we will walk, we will learn, we will endure, and we will dance. I promise. I will whisper it, as my wounded head falls upon this pillow. You will be loved, as no man has ever loved you, you will be loved as the most gorgeous creature to have walked this earth.

And as Love strokes the hair around my sleepy head and my arms mingle around hers, there is the truth about us. There is the truth about Cupid, which I must tell her. She gives me a soft kiss and all else disappears. There is a truth about Love and me. I simply must have her. Never again in the next life, I need her in this one, never again tomorrow, I need her today.

There is no existence without her, every other night would be a lie and an empty morning. Every other moment is empty and forced, just feet dragging through the mud of days. It is Love who suddenly illuminates my life, who brings peace and kisses and simplicity, it is Cupid that ravages my mind and my dreams, hunts for weaknesses in my spirit, has a monsterly taste for my soul. It is Love who completes, who sings and soothes, who brings my steps back from the danger of the edges. A love so noble and willing, so daring and true, a love that leaves me breathless and proud. She makes me a better man. I will work with fingers and bone, I will never let her down, I will never let her dismay or worry. She kisses me upon the cheek, pulls at my arms and legs and asks me where I am. She is the queen of the castle, an angel among the cold and the vicious, she is a vision of all I have never known. She is all I ever wanted even when I never deserved her.

Love is a force in the darkness. I lay beside her with all my ambitions and intentions, with all my admiration. She licks my gifts from my fingers, one by one, to keep them safe. She whispers and asks why I am holding her, why I have not let go. I will never. Love, you are everything to me.

======

I find myself sitting in the daylight, willing the hours to pass, feeling I have nothing more to do. And the hours are reluctantly creeping by, some of them, some of them dropping their minutes as if by accident, some of them stopping to tie their shoes. I am impatiently waiting to see her again. I haven't a care if the gas leaks or the sky flips. Despite my dream last night. I can not contain my happiness. When Cupid sees me he will want to rip my face from my bones. He may have my face, he can not have my heart, I muse into the silence. I have given it to her. It took but two nights. Until we meet again, and again. The dream Cupid pressed into my soft defiance, it is beginning to lose its edges, though those first moments when I was awake, the fear was immense. He knows, or he will know. I remembered Love's last kisses, the ones near my eyes, the one on my lips.

Justice went to bed with a tall bottle of wine last night, Fairness went and leaped out the window. I am uncertain of what Freedom may have done. But Love held me in her arms in the peacefulness long past midnight. I fell in and out of contented sleep with my head at her breast and her fingers uncurling my hair. We loved until it was time for her to leave. The wrenching part is walking away, if only for a brief time. I whimsically whispered that I would try not to get lost between now and tomorrow. You can't be lost, my Leo, I have found you. Her words still ache between my back and my hands.

It was Cupid's twisted need to raise the stakes, to move the pieces in the game. He sweated into my sleeping mind, so I would once again struggle with the question of whether it was a dream or a past life. When Cupid sits, he does not rest, he comes with his thighs, he fidgets, he shifts, and I didn't sleep much beneath his weight. I dreamed of the ship. I was young, barely old enough to be a man, but at the age of abandonment, the age to find my way. I may have been there like others, as servants, or slaves, as fools who would never work off their debts. Perhaps I was there as an adventurer, or a prisoner, or the victim of a lost drunken wager. There was no sense of duty, no sense of familiarity, no call of the sirens, there was no allure of returning to the freedom of the open seas.

I then dreamed of the reason, a promise I had made. To make my fortune and return. I had pledged my devotion to her. She pledged her hand and her heart to be mine. I had encountered her along the dusty straight road which lead from farm to farm, and farm to the town. I was lost in my thoughts one afternoon.

She appeared, holding nothing but an empty basket, and I fell in love immediately. Our affections were furious and innocent, our courtship brief with every sacred opportunity. We loved in secret, we loved without permission. I was a young man with a soaring heart and an enraptured soul, she quietly returned my adoration one thousand times over and more. I needed only her dusty feet and our walks, the sun in her hair, and her endearing face.

I was a young man from a family with little means existing scarcely above survival. I promised her, I would earn my way there and back, I would return by any means necessary, I would return to her, and we would be together forever. She, in turn, promised, with our first breathless kiss. She would wait until the moon fell into the sea. I would carry it back to her.

I held the promise in my hands, rolling it in my fingers, and then safely tucked it away into my shirt. We would not be waiting for the winds, so we took to the oars. I dreamed it did not take the first day, I knew it would not be a magical voyage, it would be grueling if not endless. My legs did not take to the sea. We were given orders, barked and strange, orders I struggled to follow, upon legs which struggled to keep me, and food and drink and dreams washed away into the black waters.

Most of the others had wild, empty eyes. Their hearts and minds and souls steeled by their lives on the open seas. The rest were lost and broken. And I feared which I might become. During the first hours of the first day, they seemed to wish some kind of revenge upon me, for a reason I did not know. I knew I had made a terrible mistake, but my regrets would not bring me home. It was too far now, it was lost now, too far to see, too far to swim, too far to surrender. I longed for her in my own heavy silence. I should have never left, we could have loved penniless, we could have loved without possessions.

I dreamed of the third day, the Captain was to leave his quarters and reveal himself to us. We would see the face and the strength behind the brutality. We were not to speak to him or look him in the eyes. We all stood in silence. Other than brief spits and fits of sporadic chances at unrestful sleep, we never stopped working on the ship. His face was horrible and I knew I had seen it before. Not on the ship or in hell, but somewhere, in a nightmare. His belly hung below the bottom of his captain's shirt. He reeked of rum and anger and spit when he talked. He looked upon us like dogs, he despised everyone on his ship.

Though I knew nothing of the reason, I learned that day, there, in the morning, he despised me most. He ordered that I be tied to the post, and no one was to speak to me or look at me. I was bound and told I would lose my tongue after my next word. I was left there in the sun, I was left there in the cold of the night with the spray of the waves. The second night, I wanted to cry out, I was delirious the third night. I was picturing her, her beauty, her eyes in the black sky above the deepest oceans, she was the light, she was the only light. My mouth was wordlessly working, she was whispering down to me, I know, I know, my love.

Cupid would stand over me and eat, so I would know the pain of hunger. He would drink long and spill it down his opened dirty shirt so I would know thirst. I dreamed he told me I could speak two words, and then I would be free. But I would have no freedom. He showed me the promise I had made, he had stolen it from within my shirt. He showed me the promises I had made, and then he squeezed them in his hand. I knew Cupid spoke nothing but lies.

I surrender. Those were the words he wanted me to say. I would not allow myself to. I willed myself not to. My Love. Those were the only two words I remembered and could speak. I had lost all sense of time, I had nearly forgotten my name. But my longing for her, she came to me in visions and whispered it to me. I dreamed the torturous journey continued, my mind and my memory were failing, my body weakened. My pride became a wet animal and jumped over the rail. I had the last of my will and my promise to her. Cupid was growing weary of his own games. The first mate was ordered to beat me and then was beaten when I did not speak. He sat before me, with his legs outstretched and his feet on my face. He drank from a jug, he flipped playing cards at my face. He smiled a joyless twisted smile. He said I was going to tell him my deepest fear. I was going to betray myself and my love.

It was that night, in the silence, beneath Cupid's boots,

beneath the stars, as he worked his cruel fingers into me, into my heart. I realized he had won. Cupid always wins, and he knows it. The crew was finally allowed to laugh. In the light of the morning, I was in a small boat with Cupid and six men to row. It was the final game. We stopped within sight of land. It was just as he promised. There would be enough food and drink to last ages and ages. I would be deserted and alive, never to be rescued, with the gnawing, the madness, the truth. The broken promise. I would live my days and never return.

Or I could pull the heavy chain, open the cage, and drop into the mouth of the sea monster. There were but two numbers on Cupid's favorite dice, there were but two numbers and faces on his favorite cards. Hers and mine. His and mine. His and hers.

I surrendered. I dreamed I took the chains in my hands, let myself fall over the boat. I followed them down, and there was a cage, I lifted the lid, drifted down into the icy water. I fell into the mouth, fell, and fell further, my eyes turned up, I continued down its throat, into its stomach. I was there, knee deep in the bodies and the soul, in the boil and the foam, I watched it clench its teeth and block out the light.

I awoke this morning the seafoam was thick at the foot of my bed, and I was looking for her.   The prisoner became victim, the victim a puppet, the puppet a trophy, the trophy a lovepauper. And now the narrator. For all the blind readers here, the story becomes thicker.

I am since past the filth and ashes of last night's dream, the sheets with rancid seafoam have been thrown in the garbage. My head has cleared. I sense I will see her soon. Our new hearts find one another, as though they always will, or always have. To be a soul within a soul, a desire of a soul, I now know it as a soothing drowning fulfilling unrelenting passion. A light with no boundaries, a truth accepted without a word. Exquisite surrender and rebirth. She is coming to me, I feel time and distance moving aside. This nameless day now has a face and a reason, a richness I am about to taste, a lovesmile. The hours that have passed since my fingertips last released her are gone from my memory.

Each moment becomes a desperate reunion. The past is folded and pressed and placed in the closet. There is only the present and the future. I see her face, and all the faces and voices of strangers are gone. To hold her is to know I will never be lost. The subtle way she comes to me, it's enflaming, it is a relieving ache in my very bones. I raise my eyes and capture hers, we can't see the world's debris and the universe's wreckage, we see only loveruins, and it is getting worse. She comes to me with no reason or motive, but to be mine once more. I belong to her. I belong here, to my love, to my intended. We meet with charged hearts and hands and kisses. I can not tell where my touches end and hers begin.

For me, Love has arrived with comfort and confidence. She ruins nothing and rules nothing, she changes everything. I was upon no path or journey to alter, I was on a static plain of human existence, there was no force, no flavor, no reason to rise or descend, somewhere between the shadows and the present, the present and the future. I was wrapped by the machinery that brings one day into the next. Love has come with no coarseness, no sense of need, with an unfocused softness soaking my senses, with an enveloping tenderness. She has gently wrapped a reason around the world, it spun into it like silk. I am hers, and she is mine.

I sit on a low rock wall, very much where we decided to meet. I am not early, Love is not late, we are suddenly close to where and when we needed to be. We are sudden and unexpected, and aged over centuries, centuries of longing and trust and truth. Our steps have never been missteps, our mistakes have never been our own. I gaze around through my wait. The world seems to be made of plastic, at this moment, plastic, hard and cold, perhaps not fake or listless or unalive, but two dimensional. The buildings, the trees, the breezes, even the people, they have no longing or fever. I sit and wait, wait to see her light.

Soon enough, I look to my left as though I have been coaxed, as though I have been sung to or whispered to, here she comes. Love's light approaches, I sense it before I can see her. It casts no heat, it calls me name, I hear it in my stomach and my legs. Run to her, run to her. There is no need to hurry, we have the countless hours of lovers now. Her blazing eyes and easy angel's smile appear first. All the oceans and all the fresh ink on every page and promise will dry before I tire of Love's first glance. Her hand slips softly into mine as though it were created to be there. These hands of mine are hers, for all they have and have not done. She caresses my heart, it is hers. She seeks deeper, oh this satisfaction. Love is the meat and the milk for the soul.

I am here for two hands, I am here for the safety and sanctity, the sensuality of two kisses. I am here for two hearts, for the promise and the pleasure. For the life of unbridled hope, for the clarity beyond the questions and the fog. Love brings me beyond time and the known, into a life with no secrets and fears, no catastrophe and no pain, she leads me into a garden of life. Beyond the sweltering stink and smoke, beyond the reach of success or failure, into being, the casual ease of being. Our trajectory will not be predicted or changed. Love leads me into a quiet beauty, perhaps to a world she has discovered, or a world she has created. For she has shoulders, she needs shelter, too.

There is a joy I have never known, a taste I have never known, there is an exhilaration within the absolute peace. These hands of mine are no longer crippled by work or want, they dance with desire. This long drawn empty smile is now alive. Every word I speak seems to come from beneath, beneath my skin, beneath the weight, beneath my worry, every word I speak is finally the hungry delicious truth.

We kiss again, as though for the first time, we kiss again with magic and familiarity. We kiss as lovers no longer torn, no longer empty or lost or searching. We kiss with a tenderness, in a fever, we kiss unprovoked, with the certainty of tonight and tomorrow. I will kiss you, forever, my Love. And I will wait for each one, my Leo. My hands hold hers as though they have wanted them for 500 years, my hands hold hers as though they are remembering 500 years. My lips brush her cheek, and we will never be alone again, we will never be forgotten.

We move easy down the sidewalk, we are but two in the world, we are the only two in the world. She blots out the electric lights, I can not tell if she rises to the stars or if they fall upon her. We keep a sweet luxurious pace, we are thick in our closeness, thick close at the legs and hips, elbows and arms. We have either been here before or we never want to leave. As certain as all my names I have forgotten, as certain as the memories we have both missed and captured. This woman and I, I and this woman. Held in a cloud and bursting from our secret. She possesses the movements of a spirit tonight, and I walk like a man who will never let her go. She is close at my side, closer than the past or the future, she digs in closer than this very moment.

Time has surrendered, as has fear, and the weight of

doubt. For a moment, we are perfect, and nothing else exists. I check again, in the next moment, and we are still perfect. Not as individuals, but together. Perfect enough for the world to tie its shoes and walk humbly away. We are nothing shocking, we bend easily into the night, we vanish into the light, we are an old forgotten story meant to be told. We are meant to be. They put away their shovels and let our sweetness spill, it can be cleaned up tomorrow. They gather their towels and shower in it. Let our sweetness spill. I feel her fingers tighten around mine. I feel her warmth pressing invitingly into me. I pause and move the hair from the side of her face, I send it over her shoulder. I breathe again, I breathe her stunning beauty. I bathe in it for a moment. My heart has a home, it has a place. She looks into it as though she has always known it, our eyes unlock and give our legs the freedom to move again. I will walk forever with her, I will walk to that next moment.

This new feeling and freedom, with Love, and my unburdened steps. I will sing as a man who has never known how, dance as a man who knows no steps. We will go eat tonight, as people do. She tells me of a place, a safe place she knows, not far from here. A place I have never been. She will bring me to many places I have never been. I smile like a boy in love. I do not doubt her, I doubt only the existence of a place of safety, beyond us.

Once you have the taste from the lips, you lose the feeling of going backwards or forwards, you have only the kiss from the lips.

We are seated in a place unfamiliar to me, but with her the familiarity and comfort is becoming so wrenching, so pure. I am but two days into the love of lifetimes. I nearly forgot how to see and how to speak. Love crushes me with understanding, she knows I have never learned to fly before. She wants to know about Cupid, and I don't want to lose my appetite for this meal or for the evening. But she coaxes me, pulls me softly, encourages me. The mood is silky and smooth, truthful. Love could take anything and possess everything, if she chooses. Yet she looks into me with these eyes that sing only kindness.

With no desire to do so, I tell her about Cupid. In hoarse whispers, I look down into my hands, down onto my untouched plate. My eyes remain down beneath the heaviest of my brows, the worst of brows. I can not bring myself to raise them, I can not see her go pale, I can not see her distraught, I can not bare to see her question or worry. I offer Love the most simple version of the most simply story.

I am the man Cupid ruined and ravaged the most. I existed in brutal and unacceptable ways. I was weak. I was made to be weak. I am suspect. I never asked for any of this. I have been pursued and harassed, I have been broken. Cupid has been in my life and dreams for so long I fear he and I will never part. He will never let me leave. I have asked to surrender, I have pleaded for the end of the games and mischief, for the end of the pain. I tell her of his horrible hands and his horrible dripping mouth. How I was bent just to be a bloodspot, a humiliation at his feet, a joke at the table where he eats. Love does not believe or understand, his hands fall heavy upon me, they fall dark upon me. And they fall on the rest of humanity. He has a false energy, a false light, he sings riddles and lies. He feasts upon men and women, for most know nothing of love. He offers nothing more than a flash of war, the war of flesh, the heat of gratification, of recklessness, of fleeting thrills, and the quiet remorse.

And it may be the fault of us all, with souls that no longer wander and explore and ache, souls that don't seek, souls without true hunger and home. We are stationary, listless, and we are prey.

I raise my eyes and there is sincere wetness around Love's eyes, a look I have not yet seen. You are not in a cage, she tells me, you are not in chains. Love has no limits, love has no boundaries, love suffers nothing from the moment it is held. It is acknowledged and spoken, it is felt and heard, once its fires race through the veins and the bones. Love looks upon me with eyes I have never seen and can not remember, she looks with eyes meant to be mine. They are mine and mine alone. I have seen them in the tallest grass of the past, I have seen them when I wasn't expecting them. I see them when I need them most.

Before I can speak again, the night baked air comes through the front door. It has the chill of confrontation. The moment loses its warmth, I suddenly ask Love to exit through the side door. I plead with her. I promise everything will be fine, I grip our table, seeking strength in my hands. I beg Love to retreat into the night, to escape like a secret, and she reluctantly does. My voice is almost as heavy as my heart. I tell her I will find her.

Cupid is behind me, he is with me. Cupid is all around. He is the knuckles against my forehead, the pressure behind my eyes. He is my past and present, he sits upon my future. He is an energy and a darkness in the room, he is filling it, I feel the heavy air. He says he tried to find me, in all my miserable habits and places. He has tried to call me. Where have you been, Jack, my boy. He pulls a chair to the booth that moments ago was just a quaint place for two.

Cupid has a game, a chance, his choice, a game for everything or nothing at all. I know the game is rigged. I know he offers neither chance or hope. Cupid tells me it is a rugged night outside, and I would be better off here, taking a beating, or better, follow him to a little place he knows. Cupid doesn't want me to catch a cold out there, or any sense of nonsense or bravery. He hopes I am not trying to break from the arrangement, his arrangement. With the entire world but a whisper from his whims, he chooses me, time and again. I have never been so uncomfortable with him as I am at this moment. I smell nothing but his breath and his sweat.

He tells me I am his favorite trophy. I will refuse to break and wilt, and then he wills me to surrender. But now he sees a new light in my eyes, and he can not have that. We have been at this for a long time, Jack, my boy. He leans in closer and I cringe at nearly every word. The way he speaks, it hangs across his lips, it is like death, like sausage, like grease and hatred.

The truth and horror of Cupid is for eternity, I realize he dogs and sniffs my every step. I am not safe in my sleep, my dreams are not my own. I was heavy and ripe with surrender, he could feel it. He kept me dangling on that delirious edge, he could taste it, he didn't care which way I fell. I fell into Love, I can't be certain if he knows. I have to believe it is simply a matter of time.

And against Time, me, he, we, any man, it is a lost struggle. Cupid spoke of his game and the odds are piling impossibly high in front me. He prefers it this way, the long slow rot and decay of hope and chance. Somehow my eyes have maintained my secret. He can't see beyond the past and the pale and the pain. He can kick me and pummel me, Love somehow remains safely outside. He leans in and sniffs at me, he raises an eyebrow, as if there is a new stink about me. Cupid cracks his knuckles, one swollen pig knuckle at a time, I try to maintain the appearance of the same old mangy mutt out in the yard. The uncomfortable minutes refuse to pass, the pauses are heavy. He knows something, for the first time in ages, there is something to take. It wets his cruelty, it wets his interest. Even Cupid tires of battering a man with nothing to lose. Stick around, Jack, my boy, I'll be seeing you soon. He rises and leaves the booth.

I wait, I wait for the hands of time to move again. Ten minutes. Fifteen. Twenty. I receive the check for our meal, Cupid has added a sandwich to it. I finally make my exit. I find Love, my heart is pounding in my chest. I find her in the moonlight, the rain is trying to fall into it. I wrap my arms around her and begin to say, we can only take the path we have been given. She looks at me with her swollen beautiful eyes, she holds me tight and holds me closer. She gives me a kiss I will never forget and tells me will take the path we choose. In her hands, we are free.

=====

This night is deliberately, deliciously slow, it stays draped upon us. It has us boiling happily in a stew. It is an unexpected kindness, an unexpected reward. She lays in my arms, I feel she has never left, I feel she has always been here. Not in dreams but in flesh and warmth and want. The desires of the innocent, the tastes of the innocent. Truth and fantasy and wandering satisfactions. Bring me the light, my Love, do no rise to turn it on, just bring it with you. Love with no objections, love with pure intentions. A love with a past unheld and a future unfolding furiously. Our starving mouths pressing again and again as though our kisses are in the way.

The world outside can not find us here. Tomorrow can not find us here. These hours are a lovebanquet and they are ours and ours alone. She breathes, my Leo, from somewhere on the other side of my touches. I nearly lose myself beneath her caresses, but she holds me tight. I lay still as Love rips through, quietly and sweetly, ravaging my soul to keep it safe. Heat and trust and lust are alive and unashamed in the darkness. The only sound is my hands leaving her hair and racing themselves across her skin. I try to adjust my eyes to this moment and this new life, Love closes them and tells me I do not need them anymore. Just heartfelt lovehands and lovefingers and lovespiders racing up and down the spine.

We rest, two lost and found bodies beneath a winking moon, with the applause of the stars, a festival of delights. Glorious uncontained love. I see my heart as if for the first time, within every whispered promise, and she eats them all. I am here, safe in her hands, safe in her arms, she brings me somewhere beyond rapture. We refuse to surrender to the last hour of the day, we refuse to surrender to the last minutes calling. We lay in comfort, frozen in time and place, we have not yet had our time, it is owed to us, we have not had our place, we are carving it into the universe, and it wonders why we are digging into its ribs. We have one last kiss, not for tomorrow but for the last 500 years and the next.

The angels may cry out for the lost and forgotten, they do not cry for us. We exist in a lazy haze of perfect moments, separate from living and far from dreams. We exist in moments built for two, created by two, somewhere between Time and the world, somewhere safe. There is no reluctance, no hesitation, no remorse. Just the cascade of purity, in a room, in the darkness, somehow detached from the rest of this life, their lives, our lives. The soulful savagery, the willingness, the new lovecuriousity, the lovecandy within her skin, the loveletters penned by my whispers at the side of her neck and the small of her back. Love's face has her eyes, staring back at me, it is where it belongs, closer than the other pillow.

There is a hanging distress wanting to mingle with our new hope, we rise and dress and Love must go. For tonight. She has already crept into all the tiny spaces. I am crawling with her. My fingertips hold hers until we silently part with another promise. I see it in her eyes. There is no need to speak of something we both know. She whispers you are my favorite my Leo, and I kiss her forehead goodnight. It will be hours before sleep takes my mind, my heart and soul will not be contained. I hope she is heavy in my dreams tonight, later tonight. I stay outside for a few minutes, Love is thick in the clouds, thick as honey in my head. She has left and she is not going anywhere.

I hope the hours will not be cruel and long tonight, I hope they do not take their time. I smell Love in the room. I taste Love in the room. I can not lay down. There is a future and a world lying before me. The heat remains in the bed, it is a heat, a passion for two. I will walk these floors and I will count these walls. I am at peace, I am empowered, there is new blood in my veins, there are songs in my eyes, dances in my legs, there are words in my ears. My hands are empty and my arms are anxious, Love remains a lingering touch. I will be in a loveavalanche tonight, there will be lovestained and lovesoaked thoughts tonight. I don't ask where she has been, I do not know where I have been. I will ask if she arrived safely home. Let the devils hold their own tails tonight. I have tasted rebirth, I have tasted the other side of the mystery and the miracle which laid before me. I have been brought home. My mind is in fantastic ruins and fragments, I hold my own face. She loved me here, on my face.

I confess. I have the will to walk until the weight of the past falls behind us. It will be a dead forgotten weight. I will walk until its voice isn't heard, its laugh isn't heard, until its hair is gone. It has been a long, long grueling wait, and the wait is over. I have the markings of a man who has not lived his best life, I have the markings of a man who has lived no life at all. I have the heart now of the richest man, consumed by hope. I believe the pain was for nothing and the beauty is absolute. We can leave our damaged pieces at the door. They are no longer necessary, they only make noise and weigh our pockets. We don't have to remember them. I confess. The range of my misguided steps were wide and raw, the years faded, the years unfolded. I have a new path to walk, I am using my legs which became a stranger's legs. I am using them and beginning to feel as though they were always mine. But on these stronger stranger's legs, there is an unfocused direction. There is an easy purpose, there is a destination. A walk without a beat, a walk without a pace. On these legs I can nearly dance. I can kick away the shadows. I can kick away the boots that lead me astray.

I confess I was never the man I was supposed to be. I could blame life or Cupid as the criminals. I will ask forgiveness if I have sinned, if I have stolen or harmed, neglected or deceived. If I was short sighted or ill willed or prejudiced. I will ask forgiveness if I was blatantly stupid or cruel. It may have been Cupid. Or I was never where I belonged. I was the mud behind the fence, the silence between the drips, somewhere between warmth and chill, dull and light.

I confess. I was but an angry empty cage, just days ago. Now I am open garden, an open free field, I am an open heart. Let her come through me like a tempest, let her power shine through with the final verdict. Let Love judge me. I am not an aging man I am a freed soul. Flames replace the anger, flames replace the questions, peace replaces the flames, and love conquers all. If you are in the moment, if you understand where you are, if you aren't set in some deliberate illusion, love will take you.

Love will defy and define you, crush you back into your roots, your individuality, your truth. Love will never count the steps you have taken, love cares nothing of the darkness on your shoulders or the bottoms of your shoes. Love blurs the past with the moment and with the future. Love sweeps her paintbrush. Love will have you naked and speaking.

I confess. I can not live without her now. In the simplest, quietest moments, I love her most. Her kiss is a treasure, her kiss is a reward, it is all a promise I am trying to say. She and I, we will never again live the lives we have known. Kiss after kiss, this life will explode. We will explore hungrily and breathe so heavily, and relax and delight and fall into each other, fall around each other, until we are bones and dust, until we are lovespent, until we have the apologies of yesterday, the ease of tomorrow, and the sweat and the passion of right now.

I will be happily lovedamaged, and never to be broken as I have been. I will be healed.

=====

Love and I are holding hands, walking through the famous streets, the dead streets, the hot crowded streets. We are seeking out a quiet place. She suddenly swings me around and we stand, she points to a picture. And then another. Is that you, she asks. There is a blazing flyer on a wall, and another. A couple on a pole, on a tree, they are blowing across the street, they are stuck in the gutters. Cupid is having a party, and I am the guest of honor. My strange face insists on staring back at me. I barely recognize the eyes. Her steps move on, unwavering, I follow along, feeling like I have no knees. Love stops and looks into my eyes, she kisses me as though she may have the strength for both us. I walk along beside her, not daring to let go.

I don't want to be the guest of honor. I don't want to be the trophy on Cupid's wall. Love takes my face, her hands are on my cheeks, her fingers draw across my lips and across my forehead. She touches my eyes. No, my Leo, you are mine, and I am yours.

It is a strange, ominous feeling, I am the anonymous celebrity, I am the man without the hour. No one knows my name, no one seems to recognize my face. There seems to be a humming and a murmuring. Cupid is having a party. There is only the day and the time, the booze and the food and the dancing and the massacre, the undergarments and the underlying misery. A nostalgic bash, the flyer says. Come dressed in purple, the flyer says. This city will be abuzz. No one knows my name, and no one recognizes my face. I am almost in a trance, walking beside Love. This must be the game he was telling me about. A game with no choices but final choices. A game with no chance. Perhaps this is the final insult, or worse. It seems half my life I have had no choices and the other half I do not remember. I do remember all of the dreams, he was sure to make them pure salt, and oily vinegary pain. I do remember. And I do not want Cupid to take me from her again.

Wherever we are walking, the bodies are thinning, the air is beginning to lighten. What if I am but a trophy on Cupid's wall? What if I was never meant to be anything more? If these last days were nothing more than a complicated ruse, nothing more than an orchestrated final shot across the shoulders, I don't want to know. I don't want to return again. I want no more chances. I would rather be beyond. I would rather stay in the cold and the dark. I would rather have nothing, possess nothing, feel nothing, be nothing, and lose nothing. Stolen hope is the worst hope of all.

Love becomes a mist in my eyes, upon my cheeks. Her hands are in my hair, they are upon my arms. She gives me a cool, soothing kiss. A little farther now, Leo, I follow her, her steps take us over the world, they seem to bring us through the world. I hear no sounds, I have nothing but her hand again in mine. My face must be darkened, deep with worry, maybe remorse. She gives me another light kiss and tells me to keep walking, to stay on my feet. Yes, yes, lead me past the mysteries, lead me to where the comforts are. We should run up and down the stairs and race down the halls, past the shadows, past the noise, we are not safe here, we are not safe anymore.

I am in a vice, in two heavy handed grips. One which I desire, one which I both despise and fear. Love is new and amazing, Cupid is ageless and miserable. I know where I would rather be, I know where I want to leap, I know where I want to dream. I feel my insides being torn left and right. Love and Cupid are strangers, I somehow lay between them, like some wounded prize. Love and Cupid, a force and a force, a blessing and a curse, an angel and a demon. I feel pitiful, helpless, as though I am waiting to see who wins. Lightness or darkness, tenderness or cruelty. All these years and I have no say, no control, I am as loose in reality as I am in dream.

And now there is Love's next kiss, with a new taste, a new burn and certainty. I kiss her with the want and longing of lifetimes and centuries. She kisses with a passion untold by man and legend, unknown to cultures and kings and queens. Love's fierce and sultry illuminating and demanding kisses, they bring me around the heavens, and they flatten me to the ground. She looks at me and kisses me once more and asks if I can feel it.

It has the power of the moon and the tides of the oceans, it has the fury of summer lighting, the sweet silent coating of a wet snow. This kiss upon my mouth, it speaks honestly. The truth of the ages, the pain of the past, the furious promise of days to come. Yes, I feel it, I barely remember my name or where I was going a few days ago. I want one more kiss to forget, and one more kiss to remember.

I remember there has never been a place I wanted to be so badly. I remember, it washes over me like Time. Throwing my heart as though it were made of brick and stone, and Love making it a home. I remember feelings without reward or purpose, with darkness and no one hearing my words. And I remember waking with the light of love on my face, when my movements were not methodical and mechanical, when dreams and hopes chased me from the bed, drove my hands to work and reach and seek. When love appeared as a tiny white light and became a sun.

My mouth is thick with emotions and desires I can not

speak. She blankets herself around me. She does not want me to have the days and nights, they give us nothing. She shelters me, she keeps me in her hands. The world can be the world, just as it wishes. Ours exists harmlessly, in a different place and a different time. We don't need much room. Love and I exist where only two souls touch, two souls dance, two souls share the truth and trust and lust, two souls who know the reason but not the rules. We know the songs but not the riddles, we know the wisdom of Time but not the hours and the minutes. We are the history of mankind, we are the future of mankind. We can not abide by the rules.

Soulful, true love, exists within a slice of the universe where most are not allowed to touch or reach, and none are allowed to interfere. None but one.

Love looks into my eyes for one last time tonight, to help me through this night. I hope I dream of her, I hope I wake sweating each hour. I need her and ache for her only when I am with her and without her. She is a comfort and an inspiration. I have to learn to walk on these new legs. I trust my love, she tells me to fly, she tells me to sleep though I am coming out of years of darkness. I will have her tomorrow, I will have my answers tomorrow. She seeps and drips and flows, I can think of nothing but tomorrow and what she may bring.

There is nothing more to be gained or lost. She has quieted the storm and the battle. I don't bother to pick up the pieces. I am covered with a soaking ease and a feeling of serenity. There is no violence left in the hours, I wait and I wait quietly. In the distance, beyond the window, in the city, the night cries out. But not for me, it is not mine to suffer.

I suffer only the hands of Cupid, and she told me she

will take that away, too. How and when I do not know. I know only this new strange faith. The noises have left the darkness, they have run off to disturb another man's sleep.

======

I dream of Cupid's courthouse. It is a massive, intimidating structure of white stone and cold gold trim. Most of it rose from the ground after Justice was burned. It is down close to the river, so the guilty can be quickly disposed of. Anyone doomed to come here feels it first and knows it quickly. There is no fairness here. There is no hope or chance. Nothing is said and nothing is heard. There are but accusations with no defense.

I am in Cupid's courtroom, sitting in his glass box like the next and new spectacle. And being of little wealth and means and short of friendships, I am granted a lawyer's assistance. He makes no case or objections, he has no tongue and no knowledge. He is only here to mop the floor at night, to wash away the verdicts. Cupid's face is on the prosecutor, it is on the judge, it is on all twelve of the angry jurors. He suspects I have been up to something, something that stinks, something suspicious. Something you know I would not like, Jack, my boy.   I dream I sit silently and stoically, knowing I am not here to explain myself or defend myself. I am here for the spectacle. I am here to be cattle prodded, berated, spat at, laughed at. He would gladly humiliate me, if I knew anyone in the room. It is another of Cupid's parlor games, right down to the blood on the gavel. He waits, he wants to see if I will show my hand, give him something fresh to feed upon. There is always something to be lost, something to be taken. His horrible fingers need but a chance, a moment, an inch.

I struggle to hold back my thoughts and my secrets. I think you are holding out on me, Jack, my boy. I dream of the strength to maintain the charade, I dream of showing him my empty hands. I hold and have nothing, I hold no cards, I have nothing to gamble, no way to raise or fold. I have nothing to wager. Cupid leers at me. He could take my tragedy, take my submission, he could leave me shirtless and voiceless and hopeless. I am hardly amusing to him anymore. If he has lost his interest, he could dump me in the river and be done with it all.

Cupid would prefer if I would beg or grovel. Be at least a bit of a sport, he says, be a bit of a fight, Jack, my boy. Somehow, in this inescapable dream, I give him no satisfaction. So he begins to lie to the court, for the court is his, and all of his faces are in agreement. Surely he is due for some kind of compensation, if nothing more than some amusement. At my expense.

I dream I exit the courthouse, not by the river, but down the same steps I climbed to enter. I sense the heaviness and the height of the building at my back. I sense the sentenced granted, it is around my shoulders. The sentence to be served within two minutes to years to two more lifetimes. Cupid spat on the floor before I left. He has never despised anyone as he does me, not now or then or ever.

I have been awake for some time now, whether real or imagined. I am struck by my own lack of worry, struck by the absence of the morning sickness which follows Cupid's dreams. In the quiet hours I have stumbled away from doubt. I feel the aimless lure of certainty, perhaps. I assume all of the questions are answered. I am broken and battered to the point of relief. I am emptied and annihilated and beyond sensations. This will probably be a wonderful day.

My mouth worked and twisted itself into a whisper. It was Love's magic, and if not her magic, then her force. Something lingering beyond the beauty and the passion and the enlightenment, something I can not name, something which I can not tell is within the light or just beyond. Despair is eerily absent, as is the usual sense of surrender, the sigh of a restless night, the aftermath of an invasive dream. There is no stab of a memory given and then slickly removed. There are no footprints from Cupid's victory dance. He has either released me or I am being set free. The day is too quiet to determine which is true.

The world, my world, has no edges or points, nothing to grab, nothing to tear, nothing to trip over, there are no mistakes to be made. My world has no confusion, no dread. It is not somber, there is no chill. Love rounded and smoothed the world, my world, when she kicked it over on its side. She did not intend to take my legs or make them weak. She brought the dancing of the living, the living and the loving, as if it were simple, like sweetness in a spoon.

I scarcely think of Cupid's rage and revenge, though it is possible, it may be hanging in the clouds in this very moment. The experience, the immensity, the innocence, of love washing through the opened gates, loving running wildly and consuming. The modesty of Love, the temperament, the frightening embrace of love, the undeniable irreversible hold. All goes silent, the hauntings recede, the empty faces do not appear in the darkness. There is but one face, now, one gaze, one voice, it is my favorite flavor, my favorite scent. The rest of my senses are dulled into sleeping pieces, there is but one thought, one memory. A foundation and a fire to build upon, a foundation and a fire that can not be searched for or wished for. It discovers you.

The truth and the light submit to her curves and my straight lines. And all the sultry things. The past is a bully with no menace, today sings to me from beyond the trees, tomorrow wants to join secretly in the night. I am willing to wait a little longer, a couple more hours.

The burn of this day was lost upon me, as though I staged myself before leaving. Whatever bets or promises were made will have to wait. The daylight has fallen past our reach now. I lurch from a lovetrance and feel I am hungry as evening nears. I walk outside as though the door of the cage has been opened. My legs shake the dust from my mind. There is no keeper at the cage, there hasn't been one since Love came to town.

My steps will be true, I know, my walk and my talk, my everything, they will be true. I move steadily and purposefully through the only streets I have ever known. I find I barely know them now. There is a new light in town, there is a new song. I am sure I am being called. She is my muse. I do not see the passing faces and they do not see mine. I do see my own, it is new, I see it in the windows, I see it in doors, I see it in concrete, on benches and bushes and buses and taxis. I see my face, beside my old reflection.

And those flyers drift like the dead. Everyone already knows. It is to be a Cupid extravaganza, an unforgettable bash, an invitation to be pulled meat in gowns and tuxedos. An evening of luxury and debauchery. With my old face, shadowed with sadness, as the poster boy. It seems everyone I pass has a flyer. Everyone is excited, we must, we must, they must! I pass silently, nameless and faceless, without a hint of recognition. I have nothing to gain and nothing to lose. I am the trophy mounted upon Cupid's wall, and he despises me most. It is the last play of one last game, one last broken promise. Cupid and his need for blood is rising.

I round the corner and there she stands, there is Love, precisely when and where she said she would be. And once in her arms, there is no room for anyone or anything else. She heals my broken face and my broken walk. We are together, suddenly, and alive.

=====

Love is a rhythmic beauty pulsing in my mind, she scurries through the corners and the wide opened drifts. She is in my eyes, behind my eyes. She is a welcome warmth. She gives me her fearless blue gaze. She takes nothing and demands nothing, and I offer all that I am, all that I have, with every breath and touch. We are not strangers anymore, my sweet Love and I, we are not travelers anymore. Even the wind whispers its apologies and moves along the sidewalk so we can be alone. Just the two of us. We embrace, beyond the heart and the reach of the universe. For it has done us no favors so far. We are safe from the wants of the people and the animals. Our touches rise like a fever from our hands, the evening takes a bow and gives us a few more moments of privacy.

I ask if she has seen, has she seen them, has she seen my face everywhere. She gives me a delicious kiss and says yes. I feel myself falling to the ground and then rising to the sky. I can almost hear her tell me she has a plan. She has repainted the world with a delicate softness, an easy light and truth, in shades I have never even imagined.

Love opens her hand to give me freedom I never wanted, I crawl back into it, close its comfort around me. I ask her to forgive me, I was never able to escape. Cupid was too massive. I tell her I will never disappoint her, I will never let her down. She wraps her curves tighter around me. A five hundred year loveflood washes over us and nearly takes us off our feet. Five hundred years, I may count higher, but I remember no further. We are in the wash, in the warmth, in the frantic days of new lovers. We are in the moment, we have known this before, we have known this countless times. I search her eyes for the name I might remember and realize it does not matter at all.

Our souls cannot pass each other again. We are two souls unwilling and unable to drown in the ages, two souls starved and hungry with the search. We are two souls in the wash and the confusion, we refuse to surrender a moment. Your light, my light, your trust, my trust, yours and mine and the affection and devouring attraction, the dreams and the intimacies, the locks and the chains of forever and always.

Love says she has a plan.

She has the face I have known for days. She has the face and the smile of my favorite.

Love is not blind or misguided, she is more grit than champagne, she is more flesh than silk. Love is never harsh, she is a delicacy, not a prison or an obligation. Love is not a tragedy or a convenience. It is not a whim or a gesture. Love surrounds, it pets and encourages, it watches you grow and evolve. Love suffers as you might, and then it offers the strength you need, and allows the strength you have. Love is a mystery man was incapable of inventing, love is a force in the air and a noise in the silence. Love is never an outburst or a flash, it is an immediate heat, it is a gift to the soul. It is rain upon the heart. Love has no teeth as it sensually ravages us, there is no pain, no deception. Love is but another four letter word, another idea. Love tells me she has a plan, she will tell me over dinner, with food in our hands and in our mouths.

This night is young, it is newly born, we have not had this one before. And the promises of all the nights to come, they are all new to us, they sing and howl in the distance. But first this night. I walk beside her, following her, the path is strange yet familiar. She grabs my hand, and I let her. We turn into an alley and then through the door of a diner. There are tales of hot dishes and hot coffee and warm pies written with stickers on the windows. We are the only two here besides the bored cook and the broken looking waitress. She shuffles towards the booth in the back we have chosen, we sit side by side. She looks at us warmly, she is not lonely, she calls us honey and darling and she tells Love she is beautiful. Love smiles radiantly and says she is, too.

Before long I am pushing gravy around my plate with a fork and listening to Love's plan. I admit it sounds risky, but there is no greater risk than love. You risk your past, you risk your future. Loneliness is safety, solitude is safety, and both are taking the easy way out, both are the short route. I know Love will not abandon me to the recklessness, she will not leave me to the emptiness, she is the light, and I will find my home.

I lose track of the plan through the meandering hours and the new voices and distractions around the diner. She will tell me the rest, when it is just we two, behind the safety of a closed door. There was something about the where and the why, as we agreed upon cherry pie, and drank coffee and watched her eat it. Once we are outside, I feel Cupid has eyes about, everywhere, looking for me, looking for us. We may never be free from here, we may never be alone. She tells me we will be wherever it is just the two of us. I feel like I need a beer to stamp down the coffee, and we take some back to my place. I notice the moon as we walk back, it is hanging there, looking guilty, looking like a wrecking ball. I take her hand again and we pretend we are just two new lovers. We go unnoticed by everyone as they pass, they are all in the endless search for something else.

We reach my place without incident, the hour is nearing nine without much resistance. How wretchedly slow and purposeful the hours pass while she and I are apart. I wish they would be so sluggish and forgetful when we are together. I am curious about Love's plan. She shows me a small map, it's edges are tattered and weathered and worn. I confess I do not know what I am looking at. There are no names, no destinations, there are no distances or directions.

It is not the where or the how or the why, my Leo. It is when. She has had this map always and forever, since she was a young girl. Time herself gave it to her, they met while walking. I want to understand that I was wrong about Time. Love tells me of her beauty and kindness, and of her loneliness, for she has no one to keep and no one to hold. She tells me Time was never cruel or forgetful, never vindictive, that every man, woman, and child receives only what they deserve from her.

It is when, Leo, not where or how, it is when we meet. When Love and Time met, they were each saddened by past loves, long lost loves. Time shared with her that Cupid has but one chance to destroy a perfect love, a true love, he has but one chance to ruin two souls. One chance, one arrow, one game per lifetime. For any all lifetimes. That is the rule, that is the game Cupid must play. It is the only rule Cupid can not manipulate.

I wonder how she knows. It is not how, she whispers, it is when. She has known her entire life. We have lived blind and deaf, we have lived cold and lost, it was the only way. All that matters is that we see this through, and we each see this day. The first step is to break the silence, to stop hiding the secret, and to rely upon Cupid's rage to pursue and handle the rest. I do not wish to question her plan. I am not a piece or a pawn, I am a place in her arms, a kiss on her lips. I am in her soul, she is in mine. The smile she gives me now. What do we do, now that we are inviting Cupid's teeth and claws. I ask her what is next.

Tomorrow is next, it will be our first tomorrow, one I have never known. I should be ready for anything, because the world will be shaken, the world will be astonished, ambushed, this city will grind its gears, the night will drop her robes in front of the moon. When Cupid receives his first surprise.

======

The morning has lost its last hours to the afternoon. I have wandered, I have sat, I have waited, I have paced. I have accomplished nothing so far. I awoke decently enough, knowing I should be packed and ready. I could not figure out what one brings for a soul. Not a comb, maybe a toothbrush, not extra shoes, perhaps a pair of pants and a shirt. No, just the soul, my soul. I have looked around my place for these hours, I see nothing but the ashes of another life. I have some old photographs, some childhood memories, the rest seems of no value. I have everything consolidated in a heap in the living room. It seems insignificant, even pitiful, if it were another time and another day, it might even be sad. An accumulation of years of a life, it might amount to three slow trips to the dumpster. I leave an apologetic note on the top. I don't want to be a burden. I just don't believe I will ever be returning. I haven't been told as such, it is simply the feeling. I will exit for the last time, leave the door unlocked behind me. I haven't the slightest sense of nostalgia.

I also realized I hadn't anything to eat in the place, not a bite, not a crumb. A completely clean break, not even a piece of bread. I have the photographs from a different life, my first life, in my back pocket. There was nothing else to bring into the future. What else could there be? Perhaps only bravery, or untested courage. What does a man bring? His devotion, his faith she will find the way. If I am to be believed, as the narrator, we are but two souls, two new stars in a star choked sky, and the line between us has finally been drawn. Now there is but the hot wet sensual enlightenment, the gift, the treasure. The pleasure of a soulmate, a soulmate lost and found.

I will follow Love to the ends of the earth, I will follow her to the ends of time. But maybe not on an empty stomach. Within the journey of a lifetime, there is a place for a sandwich, and maybe a beer. A soft dizzy mist has started, a cleansing mist upon this city, a cleansing mist upon my shoulders. This will be the first day, it will begin wet. The mud is gone, the questions are gone. I turn my face into it, in appreciation. I do not look back, not once. Not to the emptiness, the obligations which devoured the sadness, not to the wandering days which gave birth to the restless nights which succumbed to the wretched mornings which bottled up the darkness and the light.

In one wrenching moment, a moment Love convinced Time to surrender to her, or at least let her borrow. It all happened in one moment. Life became a promise and not a fog, an answer and not a trap, a mystery and a destination. I find myself swollen and sweaty with lovesickness and rapture. And a hunger this greasy diner can not satisfy. A soulful hunger, a centuries' hunger. I don't need stories or songs of love, I need the press of her heart and the power in her hands.

The dam has opened with a groan and I will swim in it tonight, I may drown in it tonight. Love may lead me anywhere and I will follow, not as the meek or the mild or the broken, I will follow with the intensity and the passions she was born to create. For the true love, the perfect love, it has a messiness and its own filthiness, it is uncontained, never neat and tidy. It can not be subdued, it is wild and undeniable, it is the deepest mania, the deepest comfort, it gets in your eyes and your hair, it gets around your legs and your steps. It is the worst, it is the worst, it is absolute. Within Love's healing strength, I become a stranger to my own existence, a stranger's existence. My mind, my heart, my soul, they cry out to be loveravaged, and rebuilt with tender kisses.

I am three dripping bites into a massive sandwich and an impressive portion of a tall draft beer. Any other day I would seem like a normal guy in the afternoon, waiting on the lovecarnival. Lost in my thoughts, I never checked the corners, I never checked under the rugs or the tables. But then I was told not to maintain the secret, I was told to let it go. It feels like it is sitting in the chair beside me, it doesn't want to be choked anymore, it doesn't want to be quiet.

I feel Cupid's knuckles digging into my spine, announcing themselves. I turn to find his horrible teeth spilling through the middle of his horrible smile. He is putting his knuckles into my secret, and he is enjoying it, too. He roughly pats my head, not trying to hold out on me, were you, Jack my boy. Cupid hopes I wasn't thinking of missing his party tonight. I am the man of the hour. He might even let me hit the jackpot, maybe even kiss one of his bunnies. I tell him I wouldn't miss it for the world. He laughs into my eyes and my nose. He laughs onto my sandwich. It is going to be more fun than his last valentine's massacre. Oh the bodies and the breaths and the hearts, oh what a night. There will be a lot of meat on bone, tonight, there will be a lot of misery tonight. He wants to be sure I bring my pretty little secret.

A secret kept and now released, a sweet syrupy secret spilled, a secret too slow and too scared to run away and hide. A secret too young to know any better. Now Cupid has his breath on both of us. I will play the role of the beaten and the outnumbered, the role of the lost and the losing. The man of the hour. I will come to feel the drubbing from Cupid's hands once more. He teases, this might be the last time. And by the last, he means last. He might be tired of torturing me after all this time, maybe he has found a new one to suffer, suffer with his heart and soul, because I am not as fun as I used to be. I don't amuse him anymore.

Cupid has mischief and mayhem on his breath. Eight o'clock is a good round number, Jack, my boy. I nod and submit to eight. I nod and submit to every game he has won, a lifetime of games, ages of games, games he has chosen and twisted and turned. I sit with his heavy arms upon me. Eight o'clock, for all the fingers, he stuffs his two thumbs into my ears. I wince. Maybe we will play for some real odds tonight, something permanent, Jack, my boy.

But Love said seven, we will meet tonight at seven, not a minute after. Cupid has left, I still feel I have to throw his hands off of me. He has left his shadow in the doorway. If you admit he is winning, he has already won. If you don't believe you are losing, he has already won. I sit, watching the constipated clock slowly drip the time away. The minutes have lost their way and their will, the hours want to slide down the slide.

Love has given me the freedom, I have but to act. She has given me desperation and a destination, and I sit in this chair. Time is running thin. I suddenly feel paralyzed, hoping my legs will not be fragile as glass, when I rise, or my will be weaker still. Love has left her whispers in my mind, she has left them in my ears, they rattle around inside my bones. Love will leave me footprints tonight, to follow and chase. Love has offered herself in secrets, I have but to hold them.

Seven o'clock draws ever closer, I find the courage to stand upon one leg, and now two. I walk hastily against the time, it strikes me boldly in the darkness, it strikes me harshly. I am walking fast, I can hardly believe it as it washes against my legs. What I have known and what I have not.

=====

I find I have a different walk, it carries my heart towards the light and away from the shadows. There is an unassuming smoothness, a temperature to my gait. A purpose in my steps. There is a new confidence and certainty. I am a creature of hope, a creature of pleasure, I am a creature of redemption and adventure. I am filled with promises that are finally not meant to be broken. There is no corruption, no illness, no motive playing out behind the dark curtains.

Love appears like a light, she leaps out. She is exactly where she said she would be, and precisely when. She is exactly how I hoped and dreamed she would be. She is beautiful, she is perfect. She takes my hands for a moment. My Leo, I will keep you safe, I am going to keep you, you are my favorite.

Love must know. Love, with her eyes, with her brilliance and brutality, with her honesty. The angels are about to burst from their brothels, the stars are about to break through their fences, the earthquakes are slipping through the chains that held them, volcanoes are about to sing. The sky flips over onto her belly. The universe hesitates and lets out one heavy lovely sigh. We are given our place.

She kisses me and asks if I am ready. We are on Cupid's grounds now, the gates are opened and we are just beyond the lights streaming from the windows of his mansion. There is a mulling worrying tension in the air. Here, if anywhere, we could be victims to his shifting rules, his manipulation. You don't ask the devil to play with his toys, you don't ask the devil to swing on his swingset. For now, we are a hush in the shadows. Love keeps me close.

Cupid's event and his ego provide all the cover we could ask for. The grande masquerade has begun, the unwitting and the unwilling are spilling from their cars, they are marching through the gates up the long stone walkways. Everyone is in masks, everyone is in costumes, the slaughter is simmering, the evening is threatening to boil. The strangers press inside, one by one, two by two, some in threes and fours. The masks may hide the shock, the masks won't conceal the morning or the remorse. The parade continues, pressing, pushing, threatening to blot out the light.

I am the trophy on Cupid's wall. I am the man of the hour. I am the most despised. I will be the distraction if the laughter pauses, if the drinks begin to warm or run dry. I will be the distraction before his arrows begin to fly and find their marks. Before his fury drowns out the frenzy, before his rage drowns out the music. Love touches my hand. I am the prize which will not arrive.

She points, and I watch as Cupid's men surrender their posts, one by one. The first ones from hunger, the next from boredom, and finally curiosity gets the rest of them. They leave the gates, they abandon the cars, they forget the dogs in the yard. They press their faces to the windows, licking at the lights, wanting to taste the decadence and destruction within. They salivate over the scraps falling and dripping from Cupid's plates, from his table, from his fingertips, over the wine sloshing from the glasses, over the women hanging from the chandeliers, the dancers atop the furniture. Cupid's men, to the last, losing their way and losing their senses and duties, captivated by the bloodbath in the mansion. Strangers deliberately feeding upon strangers, the weak and the wild, the sinister and the mild, with Cupid's booming applause and approval shaking the very foundations.

Love leads me from the trees, I follow her blindly, I follow her faithfully, as I would through the years, for lifetimes, across oceans and mountains. The purity, the wildness and recklessness of Love, the fever we can reach and stand just on that edge. This is the moment the sadness and the punishment vanish. The moment belief takes over in the present and rains down upon the past.

Love's hair is in strands, her eyes are ablaze. I kiss her once, because the moment is too strong and too powerful and too perfect. We stand on either side of Cupid's car, the last one in the line. We have flattened the tires of the rest. And as two souls that may have done wrong, we have not sinned. We steal Cupid's favorite car.

Love is at the wheel, she tells me to hang on. I squeeze her hand, we have stolen his car, and now we will steal this night. She presses the gas and we head off into no particular direction, we have no true destination. It is she and I, somewhere between now and then, somewhere between now and a dream. There is light traffic, there are few eyes, there are even fewer eyes that care or that will remember. She is aiming towards a highway neither of us have traveled. I ease back into my seat, the car roars and hammers along. The lights seems to nod, and now the trees seem to salute. We manage to leave the city, I can not remember the last time I was out of its reach. A long wash of days that might have been years. But Love is not an escape, she is an experience. She has waited for me, and I for her, and now she waits in want. We will kiss after driving, we will kiss after riding, we will kiss after stealing away. The kisses will hang upon my lips like a meal, like a promise, and the fever of our embraces, as we press heart to heart. Sometime between now and the morning, I hope they will come, and I will wait.

I don't check her speed, I don't check the clock. We are racing through the soft belly of a countryside, it goes back to sleep as soon as we pass. I leave my mind unfocused. There are no guardrails, no reasons, on this road. She leaves the windows down, the night rushes past, cleaning my face, cleaning my eyes, cleaning my smile. These roads are unknown to me, perhaps to her as well. We will travel, and should there be ladders, we will climb, and should there be walls, we will seek refuge. I don't know where we are, but we are well beyond the past, the past which means nothing now. We are somewhere between the night and tomorrow. There are no sins between us, no arguments, no harm. There is but the light, the softness, and the future that awaits. The future that sleeps. I have a vision of a time with no claws and no teeth, a time with no malice or vengeance.

The world is out there in the rushing silence, let it sleep, we don't need it right now. I am sure there are angels out there, and all the inhabitants and the strangers, the animals and the ghosts, I wish them no ill will. We don't need them right now. I have Love at my side, I am in a dream from which I will not wake. I see her smile in the darkness, I place my hand on her leg, she lets her long hair sail out the window. The prisons and the doubts and the past have disappeared, dreams will become hopes and hopes will be dreams. There is nothing to suffer but waiting for the next smile. She tells me we will stop in a few hours, she knows a little room where we can stay. I have no where else to be.

Eight o'clock has long since passed, and certainly nine and ten have chased midnight right out the window. Eventually Cupid's eyes would have risen from his delicious slaughter, they would have regained their focus. He would have wondered where I was, where I have been. He would have realized I was not there, not in costume, not in character. I was the man of the hour, the trophy on the wall. He would have stopped the music, stopped the dancing, he would have even stopped the suffering. His shock would have disappeared in moments, replaced by his anger. His men would have removed themselves from their perches at the windows. They would have seen the dogs were loose, they'd gotten into the trash, gotten into the hearts and the undergarments. They would have finally seen the cars with the flattened tires, they would have counted to seven and seen one was missing. They would have faced Cupid's wrath.

In the dim grainy space within our speeding car, I can perfectly make out her endearing, enduring profile. I give her one soft kiss on the cheek. Do not move your arm from mine, do not take away your sound or your scent, do not freeze your smile, do not close your eyes. I want you in the light as much as I want you in the dark. We have stolen Cupid's car, but that is not why we run tonight. We run to find our place.

I wonder how quickly Cupid will put the pieces together. Once he clears the rooms and clears the grounds, once he searches the corners and the closets, once he has had his satisfaction and the victims and the revelers have been shoveled out in piles into the night. When the mansion is empty and the music of the massacre has stopped. And I am not on his wall. No one dares Cupid, no one crosses Cupid, no one tests his will or his hands or his patience. No one defies him, no one challenges him, not to cards, or swords or dice, not to revolvers or jacks. No one butts foreheads with Cupid, no one wrestles him or defies him. No one tests whether they are stronger or more cunning, no one wants to know if they are more deceitful or cruel. And I would be the least likely suspect, having been beneath his thumbs for so long. Cupid is the long shadow I have slept beneath, and now I feel warm.

Love drives steadily, deeper into the night. This is not our night, we won't claim it or name it. We disappear into its arms. I don't believe she is doing this as a show of will, or a show of fight or defiance. This is not a test of time or a test of strength. It is not acknowledgement, it is not forgetfulness or forgiveness. It is for the easy patient excitement, the slow wistful urges. It is for the crushing freedom of two hearts. It is because we are tickled, we are satisfied, we are starving, sitting side by side. It is the truth and the allure of the day and the night. We have no regard for distance, I am but inches away, and closer when I reach for her. We have no regard for distance, we have gone miles and miles. We can't feel the years behind us, they fell asleep with the night.

We are a few hours ahead, with no destination and no direction. I feel even Cupid can not find us now, not this fast. I hold my head out of the window for a moment to feel the weight of the moonlight. She pulls me back with one hand and gives me an unbearably light kiss. We ease into a sleepy place, where we can share these arms and legs, for at least a little while.

=====

We are in a suffocatingly small, nondescript room, a room we were never meant to be in. The darkness can't come through the keyhole, and I have Love's whispers around my neck, they are in my ears, in my mind, they are stroking my hair. I see the world within a new flash of light. It is coming. I rest and breathe easily. I am an unemployed scarecrow, I am as solid as a lamppost, shining upon his volumptuos beauty of a bride. She kisses me with nostalgia, she kisses me with no past and no weight. I would like to stay here. This is love with no regrets, love baking in the heat of a still night, love beyond the moonlight. Love in simplicity, a nurturing love, without the hold of alphabets or numbers. I lean naked into a love of understanding and acceptance.

We are lifetimes from where we have been, we are in the peaceful silence of knowing where we are. A carnal aching love, slick like the morning, a love soaked with want, a tireless devoted fortress, an endless force resting upon another kiss. A delirious love in the dash of the colors of spring, in the long days of summer, in the dawn of autumn. A hopeful love within the confines of winter, in the spit and the chill of the cold.

Love tells me of a dream of a modest gray house, a place built just for two.

It is on a road in a small town, a home made for two, we leave our shoes outside, and our footprints and loveprints are inside and they are everywhere. There are no shadows, there is no doubt and no cold. There is a light, a sense of etenity, an understanding that permeates the walls. The beauty outside in our gardens, it invades our opened doors. It swells beneath the floors, it lays its stomach on the rooftop, it takes our hands in the morning, it chases us to bed at night. The beauty without becomes the beauty within.

We do not know how and where, but when, my Leo, she says, they may chase us, they will never capture us. They will never corrupt us. Let them try with all their legs and all their breath.

I am ensnared in a moment I never anticipated and may never understand. But we will chase away the world's steel, we will chase away its dust. We will chase away the voices and the demands. There is a light between us, the pleasure lives in a heart and a soul that is suddenly free. We will live beyond wisdom and expectations. I need but a kiss, she needs but a dance, and we will have it all in a minute.

I believe I can hear a scream, a cry, it is from Cupid, from a great distance. It is muffled, swollen, it comes from an unkept animal, perhaps not a force. I have no idea how far we have traveled tonight. I have no idea how long we waded knee deep through the ages. Or it may have just been a dream. I awake with a cushioned fall. She tells me she has heard nothing. I will sink a little deeper, the road disappears beneath the car and behind the car. I will rise with you tonight, I will take us in the moonlight, I will take us in any light we are provided, any light we may find. I will take the secrets from the depths of your lips. I am the happiest man alive. If we are to be just a man and a woman, I want to be with Love. If we are to be free souls in the night, fires and hearts in the sky, memories found and memories made, I want to be with Love. If we are but a moment, a moment to wait for and hold dear and true, if we are a meeting in the breeze, forced by the days, forced by the seasons, if we are but a moment in the cruel mathematics of forever, I will take a kiss, I will take this.

Love turns us completely around and we are heading back to where we just were. She is following a map, or following the wind. I raise an eyebrow, and then realize, this is not where we have been. There is nothing behind us, everything waits before us. We have never been where and when we have needed most to be. I suppose she is right, I have never known her to be wrong. Things do appear different, in this new direction.

Time has her own way of unfolding the road, whether it is delicate or passive, subtle or aggressive. I am just a willing passenger. Time serves no one. And we apparently are on her road. She does not serve the bold, or the greedy, or the priveleged. Time serves only herself, though it is said she looks kindly upon the humble. We are the humble, Love and I.

Love's eyes are fixed upon the road and my eyes are fixed upon her. We are not burdened by the where or the how. We are rooted in the now, the floating, soggy, foaming now. We have not enjoyed or destroyed any past. We wait for the future, Time leaves a tantalizing scent. There is no coldness, there is no right or wrong, there is no pain or sorrow. There are our kisses, our souls' reflections, our mirrored embraces. There is the light in the day she creates, the marks upon the days she makes, the stars she etches into the sky with her thumbnail. Our wandering path, we are lovers, hand in hand.

We are beyond the anxiety of our journey's first day, we are beyond the treachery of eternity's first minutes. She said I am her favorite. We are beyond the trappings of the human experience. We never suffered the fear, the panic, the refusal, or the slow disastrous drip. We are but two souls, nothing more special than spectacular or magnificent. Love and I, soaked through the clothes, soaked to the bones and the truth of the want of centuries. The idea brings my kiss close to her ear.

A long sun soaked afternoon has been blown out like a candle. We stop for the night, in another town I can not name, a faceless tired town, but there is a place to have a meal and a drink on the patio. I lean over the railing, looking up into the sky, wondering what promises this night may hold, what secrets this night may reveal, or keep.

Love rejoins me, she wraps an arm around my waist. The Night gives us her eyes, she gives us her smile and her caress. She and Time, Night and Time, they slowly dance together, and give us permission to do the same. Tomorrow can watch from the silence, it has been put out into the yard like a dog. For now it is just Love and I, in a kiss peppered with breathlessness, Love and I, in the comfort of our hands.

=====

In the middle of this swollen night, I lay restless in a strange bed, listening to the sounds of Love sleeping. Our touches have escaped the covers, they have escaped the bed, they are running around the room. The satisfaction lingers between us, somewhere between her breathing and mine, in a hot place between my knee and her elbow. She does not leave me restless, she does not make me restless. It is a poison made by another. There is nothing but the slow drift between us, as we rise and sink towards one another, there is nothing but the pure pull, the ache.

Ours is divine, it crashes in furious waves, it consumes, it is a heaven I have never tasted. A whisper evolves into a key and a storm is unlocked, unleashed, held within our arms, pressed tightly between us. The air, this darkness, this unknown room, the night, they are all saturated with fingertips and kisses. New kisses. I lay, lovebruised and lovebattered, hours into the glowing after, hours into the glowing bliss. My chest and ribs and hips, pummeled into a freedom, into a natural freedom. I am free to experience, I am free to explore.

The old fires never burned so deep, they never smoked

and smoldered so richly, so exquisitely. A taste of love never to be forgotten. I lay in the silence, lovestreaked, with lines across my body, there are loveaches in my muscles. I have a long hair at the corner of my mouth that I have not bothered to remove. I keep my hand upon her bare side. I bask in loveexhaustion. I feel it in my eyes, in my shoulders, in my scalp. My hands tingle beneath her features. My heart shivers for her every sound. I lay, nearly loveparalyzed, I am love driven, lovepulverized. I lay in the divine aftermath of two souls colliding as humans, two souls dressed as a man and a woman, two souls dressed in robes.

The quiet wraps its weight around the bed, and the darkness joins. I keep my touches soft and unassuming, Love is relaxed and sleeping and absolutely glowing. I am careful with her hair as it searches across my pillow. I take greater care with her heart beating and pounding in my ears. I am lovedrowned, lovedelicate. I rest in a glow, suddenly aware I am no longer a wanderer, I have a hunger with a source. I am awake, my arms reach for what I sense and feel, for what I taste and smell. Days will bring the nights, and nights will nourish the days. I pull a soft hand, bringing it from Love's shoulder all the way down to her feet. This is where I will love. She sighs in her sleep, and I am in a place I have never known. There is a trust and a warmth and the secrets are all kept safely. We are not the animals, we are the spirtiual beasts.

I am lovehidden, I am lovebaptized, I know a peace I want everyone else in the world to experience. I lay, breathing in the entire room, the air, the light, the closeness, she sacrifices to save me. So I might save her. I am lovebound, lovechained, in this tumultuous peace. I am a man who has possessed nothing, I am a king in this world. There is not a vault to rob, a purse to steal from, there is not a pledge to make or a deal to break, there is nothing to lose or accomplish, nothing worldly can create this feeling.

I am lovesuffocated. I am loveconsumed. I ease closer into her arms and she wraps them as if she were expecting me. She whispers the words, she will take me in a dream, perhaps tomorrow. I hold her hand as she sleeps, I feel I am borrowing begged time. I rest quietly and easily. I lay beside her, knowing my entire life, I have not been the man I was supposed to be. But now, Night and Time have come together, and shown me Love and all the sultry things.

=====

Love is wearing the corsage of the morning, nothing more than the blanket from the bed and the smile on her face. We drink coffee, I debate myself over the softness of the light, and whether to speak of my dream last night. We are in the comfortable silence lovers share, in the comfort they may know , even in a strange bed, a strange place, a place not their own. We are too new to have our own. We are too old to worry. She says we might need eggs, and sausage or bacon. It confounds me for a moment, we must surely be pursued, feverishly pursued by now. And here we are, glowing with the night, talking of a late, easy breakfast.

I discover I am a fast learner of lovespeak. She speaks clearly and without fear, without mystery or riddle or ridicule. Without accusation or pain or distrust. She touches my face. Whatever you want. She speaks as though she is singing, she sings the truths, my ears recognize the fabulous beautiful colors before my eyes can see them. We bring the brilliance and the satisfaction of the night, along with our heavy breakfast, to the car. Love starts the engine, I am certain there is a fury and a confidence behind her sunglasses. I find I am more unaware of our whereabouts and direction than I was yesterday. But she does not need to ask if I trust her, I do without question, with all my heart and soul.

We ease onto the highway, we are a blaze and a whisper. She chooses music today, and music it is. There are some truths to the tales of the road. It can be endless, wandering and faceless. It can lead you or it can be led. It can be your chosen road or a path long spent and burned and deserted. It can be followed or forgotten, made or named or meaningless. I will leave it to her, as she finds the gas pedal.

I leave it in Love's hands as the sun bakes through the windows. I would rather focus upon the images and hands and memories of hands and lips not misplaced, the words not spoken or misspoken, of beddings filled and spilled and torn aside, or raging tender kisses, of breathless eyes searching for more in the darkness, in a room so dark and empty, a bed so full. We could see only by skinlight. I prefer to imagine Love's bold and subtle perfection, her patient pleasure. The car and the world and the worry are not mine.

I am again lost in another day, surrendering to her and us completely. I assume it is the minutes or hours, it is not the miles, it is the wind knocking and knuckling hard through the windows, knocking the memories of the dream I had into pieces. Beyond the heat of the night, and the cool wrapping aftermath of the morning. The tranquil sleep I encountered, the pain of the dream was at the back of my throat. I felt it in my joints, it followed me when I rose to the bathroom, when I was stumbling around the unfamiliar room.   Love's hair and singing fly out of the opened window. I hesitate, still, to tell her of the dream Cupid invaded me with last night. He ambushed me. It was a dream suffered in the stillness which awaits just beyond relief and restlessness. A dream which did not belong in the weight of our room. A dream which I find more in tatters and less clinging, each time Love absently lifts and reaches a hand and touches me.

We both understand we are not yet free. We are pursued. I dreamed of Cupid's long, devastating and horrible pursuit. His relentless pursuit he would have never abandoned even if Love and I had surrendered. I dreamed of Cupid chasing us across the lands, across the ages. chasing us on trains, chasing us on horseback, chasing us through fields and forests and deserts. We did not lead, we were pushed and pursued, to the brink of exhaustion, to the promise of destruction and rest. I had no choice but to let go of her hands. I left her in a safe place. I willed the pursuit to focus upon me and me alone. I swore I would return. I kissed her hand and gazed into her eyes. I gave her my soul, I gave her my oath, I would come back for her. I left her in the safety and the emptiness, I took the long treacherous path up the mountainside, to endure the snow and the frigid winds, the silence and the solitude. I hoped they would tire and weaken. I would make my way to the mystic Pacific and doubleback, I would elude them all and return to my Love and we would find our way home.

Love suddenly pulls the car to the side of the road. She has found a place where it is raining. There is no steam from the highway, no objections from the ground. It is a solid, cleansing rain. Step into the rain, my Leo, let it feel you.

I climb back into the car, perhaps feeling more wet than

clean, more aware than wet. But the dream has left my mind. We ease back onto the highway. I have apparently lost another day, there is a stunning sunset in the distance. I don't believe we can run forever, I don't believe we want to. I don't believe we can run much longer, not in Cupid's car, not on these legs, not without wings.

She points to a line of six familiar vehicles on the other side of this lonesome highway. Six cars with six drivers and six sets of repaired tires. This is Cupid's heavy, clumsy pursuit. If I had thought I had the strength, I would have stood up and challenged him long ago. I would have pressed my wagers if not my talent, pressed my urges if not my vinegar.

Love banks hard to the right, down a two lane road. She turns the lights off and seems to navigate either by faith or memory or inspiration. She tells me we will be there soon, she does not explain and I do not ask. I feel there are greater forces in the current I am carried within. There are eternal, immaculate, perhaps harmless forces. I will sail along because I can not swim, and I know Love will do me no harm.

We must be close, I sense she is relaxing, I sense her ease. She turns the headlights on a again, we coast to a stop in a driveway in front of a quaint house. I understand, this is her house built for two. The front is unlocked and opened as if expecting us. I ask nothing, this place feels like it has more answers than questions. I do not need to know how we arrived here, or who lives here, or if Love has lived here. I am lovedrawn, lovesmitten, love taken, it begins at the door. The loveboil rises from the ground, the sky swallows the steam as it reaches the rooftop. Here, love removes the mystery, the rambling heartaches, love is the center and the focus, it is beating red, pulsing a deepest blue.

This is the house built by Hope. Love shows me around the rest of the home, there is a plain and vibrant pleasantness, a comfort just beyond certainty and warmth, a welcome without a whisper, a hug without a touch. There is a beautiful feeling within the walls, and outside as well. It would be easy to remain here, it would be easy to gracefully and gratefully grow old here. Love tells me that Time spoke to her about this place, and Hope welcomed her. She promised it would be a refuge in a time of greatest need.

For even Hope needs a place of rest, a place of peace. Hope is eternally kind, eternally patient, she too may grow temporarily weary. She requires a sanctuary, a passive passage, delivery from the universe and the pleading hearts and the tugging hands. Love leads me to the patio outside, I am taken with it immediately. I could remain here forever. Love tells me she has known Time since she was just a young girl, and she has known Hope nearly as long. Hope, as is her sister Time, are misunderstood by the world, they were misunderstood by me, I judged them poorly and harshly. Hope is not fabulous or fashionable, she is not luxurious, she is not unapproachable or cold or icy to the touch. Hope is eternal, she is modest and demure, she is eternal without being boastful. She is immense, and she can appear as the slightest flickering flame. She is free to any pursuing heart. Even hope needs her own little corner, a place to grow a rose, a place to gaze at the stars. A place without worry or reflection.

And it is here we sit, Love and I, on a lovely patio at a small table, suddenly no longer pursued. I feel the moments of freedom, the urges of freedom, and I wonder aloud if we should not just stay. Love assures me we could remain in this embrace and never leave. But not this time, not here, not today or tomorrow. We can not allow them to find this place. We have a day, perhaps two at the most, and then we must leave.

I ease further into my chair, I am pressed back a little further by Love's heavy certainty. Not for an instant do I doubt what she believes and knows. She asks for a kiss, and I kiss her the only way I know how. I kiss her early and long and late, I kiss her in between, above and below. She opens her eyes again and shows me her beautiful smile. We are getting so close, my Leo, we are nearly there. I must trust her, I must be patient a little longer. Patience.

Patience is a newfound pleasure. It feels exotic, smooth and strange in my hands, I rub it against my forehead, across my cheeks and my temples. It is a fantasy of the past, and now it sits with me. Patience after a lifetime of waiting, after countless years with the numbing slow steady drum of waiting. Waiting for the day to drop, waiting for the night to lunge, waiting for the world to lose its way, waiting for the universe to turn inside out. Patient I can be, I am forced to be no more. Waiting for the tomorrows, the years, the beginning, the end, waiting for thirst, for hunger, for any sensation at all. Waiting for a ship in the desert, for a mermaid in a snowstorm, for the heights to fall and the weights to flow. I am here, with her, I wait for nothing, I will never leave, I can be anything.

I am her Leo, she is my light, and the realization that Cupid despises us most, he has been at our heels, deep into our footsteps. Yet no where near our hearts. The very point of his cruelty has been at my back, in my back, I have tasted his wickedness, I have swam in it, I have dreamed of his menace.

Tonight we belong here. I have faith tomorrow will appear as it chooses. We bask in the satisfaction of here and now. We are lovers who know nothing of stones and cold. We are lovers in the house that Hope built, and perhaps Time protects. And even if the bliss is fleeting, it shall be bliss. We will call each other by our names, or call each other with kisses.

Love and I find a bed in a room in the house. It feels as though it were placed here for us. The door is closed, the world remains outside. I have never known this before, and I will never forget. We share the delight of a first kiss again. Love wears red and asks if it is my favorite. Yes, you are my favorite.

I am drifting into an unfamiliar weightless sleep, a sleep with dreams or worries or regrets. A timeless sleep beyond the reach of the lifetimes, with no arms or legs, no voice or opinion, with only a free and full easy heart. In a bed with covers that lavish me like a king, I lay still, with my hand on the hip of my queen, in a bed in a room that knows no shadows or chill. This room knows no sudden cries, this room in the house that Hope built.

======

In an unseen hour in the night, Love whispers, Time had the idea, Hope created the plan, and their sister Temptation is the bait.

======

Morning arrives softly, apologizing for ending our night, but it comes with no horns, no teeth, no crashing parades. It arrives subtly, without a sound, without a splash. I sense myself slowly becoming aware of my surroundings. They do not feel so strange. And I welcome this morning, I will relish it just as I did the night. I have never known the peace of this moment. There is no need for strength or will, my movements are syrupy and fluid. This must be what forever feels like. There is no urge to hurry, I am not to be lost or found. I am exactly when and where I want to be. I have no idea of the time or what day it is. Love is beside me, still dressed in red and she is beautiful.

This peaceful morning is trying to sit upon the night, it tries to press it out of the room while the embers are still smoldering. No need to hurry for us, no need to worry for us. With my face and mouth raw with delight, my head split in two, my chest is out of the covers, my heart is beating new. My hands are upon her legs, remembering the night. I wait, simply wanting to see her eyes open. They slowly do, there is the blue. Good morning.

I don't care what color the sky is or what this day is named, if it is raining or cold, if the stars missed their buses or skipped school. I don't care if the spoons are stirring the clouds, if the knives are shaving the trees, if the forks are eating the mountains. Love looks at me and truly smiles. Good morning.

We have made the coffee, and by the way we sit and leisurely drink it, by the way the day hangs upon us like old friends, we are not leaving today. The pursuit of yesterday and tomorrow have been paused. Love touches my arm, no one has ever looked at me this way. The sweetness of the dilemma, at the house that Hope built. The world is silent and unseen, it is behaving itself beyond the yard, beyond the fences. Hope perhaps makes even the chaos behave. I am in the daylight of a daydream. There is no weight in these legs, no weight in these feet, the urge to pace is now the urge to dance. I have to taste the air, I taste it twice, happiness is light and it tickles the throat. It is beneath Love's footsteps, it lifts her from the grass.

Love wants to plant roses here, before we leave. We surround the house with them. We fix the shutters, we mend the fence. We feel the house breathe and grow. With dirt on our hands and the day around our shoulders, I finally ask about what she whispered in the night. Without a stammer or hesitation, Love asks if she may keep a secret from me, for just a few days. We have no secrets, we tell no lies, that is the promise. I stand from the new rosebeds, I wipe the soil from my knees, I wipe the soil from my hands as best I can. With one gentle finger beneath her chin and my eyes buried in hers, I whisper yes.

I found you within the rain and lightning of a dream, an impossible dream, an impossible chance. You have ensnared me, you have devoured me, you seep through the cracks within me. You color the light, you flavor the passion, you have hidden away the darkness. You have named me, you have hung my other name on another man. You have searched for what I have found. I will take the moments, one by one, not in an avalanche, not in a greedy pile, not in an inferno. One by one, gripping each, being gripped by each. You are the reason on my face, at my soft neck, in my hair. You are love beyond the tragedy, love beyond the celebration and the pagentry, beyond any failures, beyond any words.

I am intricately woven into Love's embrace, this bare threaded soul. I'll never be afraid when our steps take us long into the night, long past the night.

Days ago, I possessed little more than empty days and

hollow nights and Cupid's wagers. Today I am free. I mean for my Love to be free, loosed like water, like a fever. She sighs, standing in bare feet, her hands are at my face, they smell like earth and care and roses. Her eyes do not lie. A different man would not allow her secret to come inside with us. We wash our hands and make a meal together, sleep is waiting outside the windows. We are new and possibly terrified, in the house Hope built.

Love speaks with an earnesty, in a hushed voice, I feel her words as though they are the truth, smashing upon the rocks. She has known them all, Time and Hope and Temptation. They were born in the oceans of man's universe, they were conceived in the tides, hidden in sultry mystery. They were not born to face the assumptions and prejudices they face now. Their sole purpose was to spread their light. Whether it is the fault of man or evolution, we seek to control or outlast Time, we seek to reverse and erase the wisdom she spreads across our faces and our bodies. We seek to defy Time, though Love assures me she is harmless and helpful.

And Hope, we do not dare to hold or believe in, for she may be lost, she may meet our demanding dreams. Hope and her serums and her cures, her light and her strength. It is strange and precarious, how some have come to try to live without her. Hope, within her simple gowns, she never arranges or rearranges or tears everything apart. She is a constant, a call, a beacon.

Temptation has had the most difficult path of the three. She was created as a gift, a reason, a whisper in the silence. She is not savage or cruel, she is no burglar, no villain. She can drive the heart and enflame the mind. What happens to those who wear her kisses is up to them. Temptation offers only the hint and the limit, the idea and the magic. She is but a sauce and a flavor, but she is a spark, an eternal spark.

The three of them despise Cupid, just as much as he despises us. They loathe his cheap parlor games, his cruelty and his wrath. They have all stood just beyond the kingdom of the immortals, just beyond the palaces and the playgrounds. Cupid, over the ages, has muddied their names, muddied their gifts, for his own amusement and his own tricks. He has attempted to court all three, without success. They find him masochistic, barbaric, they have witnessed his games for centuries. Since man has learned to walk and talk, they have resisted his empty flattery.

I am not sure why now. Why they have decided to help. Perhaps Love is a sister, perhaps she is the fourth. She assures me she is not. She was simply a sad little girl befriended by them. A sad girl who grew into a woman, and they decided to help. She confesses she has never known Cupid, she has never met him. But she believes she led lives which ended not with sorrow but with emptiness, and Cupid may have been the reason. Each time I was broken, she was not allowed to be whole. Each time I was taken, hidden, misdirected, mistaken, she was not allowed to be found, she was never allowed to find me.

======

Love whispers into our night. Her secret will do me no harm. I find her in the darkness, without opening my eyes, I give her my favorite kiss. I know.

I was here in the day, I was here in the night. You will be lovesoaked, you will be loverich. With all the promises kept safe, and your secret kept safe. You are not on a pedestal, you are in my hands. I feel you writhing and real in my heart, the numbness and the sadness are gone. The beleagured and weak are not in our bed. I sense we will be leaving this house, I wrap my arms around you for another memory. I believe we will return one day, but not in madness or a dream, they have no place here. But in a spring of kindness, a summer of dedication, or autumn of freedom, sweet delicious delicate freedom.

The moon is somewhere beyond the curtains and your head and your hair are strewn across my chest. I will not move. I will kiss you in the hours lost between night and morning. I will kiss you in our hours. My kisses are hungry and reassuring, they are undisturbing. I kiss for the lives we have never known and the lives that have been taken from us. I will kiss you once more, for this life.

Love is wrapped deeply around me, she does not wake, she coaxes me to sleep. We will have tomorrow, we will have all the tomorrows. Be still, we will run tomorrow. A love without burden, without a doubt or a frown, a love like a river. She is my greatest escape from all I have learned and known. She wrenches me from that light to grow into hers. A strand of her hair is in the corner of my mouth and I keep it there. This night dance, my eyes slowly close.

=====

Night whispers her sweet apologies to us, she can no longer keep us. The day is already stretched long outside. I can tell by its body language we must leave this happy place. This day has long legs and feet that don't mean to trip us. But its hands are out, its arms are sweating, it is already working. It is time for us to go. We put away a few dishes, pull the blankets gently across the bed and smooth them. It will be as though we have been here, it will be as though we have been here for a thousand years. And have not. I do not know the exact time or what day it might be, I know only our peaceful stay here is over. For now. We are in the car and each new bend in the road takes us further away.

There was no burning, no remorse or suspicion, no vinegar, to the morning. Love needs her secret. We are in the car, I am mostly sitting, she is driving. There is nothing between us but the truth. The day hangs in clouds beyond the windshield, it hangs above the highway. The highway has no words, it is sleek and black and flat. It offers no promises and no romance.

I will miss the ease of the days we spent at the house Hope built. I will miss seeing Love in a dress, barefoot in the grass, singing to the flowers, touching the flowers, dancing with the pixies. I hope I will have those days again. Love was the reason behind the peace, she was the reason for the fever. I touch her hand to tell her I will remember her blue eyes and long hair last night. I will never forget. She smiles to tell me I am her favorite.

Love brings us barreling through long and lonely nameless miles. I am willing to pay the costs for such tenderness and delight, I will suffer for the freedom, if I must. I am not sure if it is begged or borrowed or owed. But I know, with her, there will be no such demands. There will be no regrets, no shame, no volatility. Just a feeling that knows only one place in this world. I run my hand through my hair, I run my hand through her hair. I have lived in this world for decades and decades, it has chosen just these last days to finally turn upon its head. All I need is the moments in her arms, the moments in her light. She looks at me. Yes, I feel it, too, the heavy footed pursuit.

I have known all along the insult and the harm would not go without at least an attempt at punishment. For we have mocked Cupid, we have defied him. I haven't seen his horrible face in the longest time. I can't deny it hangs in the air like a second moon. Cupid is craving revenge and destruction, his fingers want to pluck us from the candybox. Let it just be me and mine alone. We speed down the highway, I hope we are heading to a place where we will have a chance. Nothing has been familiar since this morning, nothing has appeared promising. But I am just riding. Nothing has seemed threatening. Love told me what is important is not where, it is when. I have not known where we have been since we left the city in Cupid's car. In different circumstances, I would be content and blind and ride with Love forever. I have the feeling we are heading to a place where we don't belong. And the rumblings of Cupid's war machine is somewhere behind us.

I will believe our destination does not matter. Love softens the edges of a room, she softens the sounds and brings the light. We can run until tomorrow, and then to the next, but eventually tomorrow will not come. I am determined, though, to stand between them and us, to stand between her and whatever and whomever will come. Love must be free, even if she is not mine, she must be free. She will always be mine, and I hers. We pass beneath a bridge, and something is changing the sky. In the distance this long bold afternoon is surrendering to dark clouds. Perhaps it is time to stop and rest, perhaps we have traveled enough today. Or do we drive into the storm.

I feel many miles and many hours have passed beneath the steps of yesterday. Between now and yesterday, the simplicity and the serenity of yesterday. It is too fresh, too strong of a taste to be a memory. Pieces of yesterday still hang upon me, I can smell them on my hands. Yesterday I could dance, I could walk. Today is about me like flying bugs. I will see what these legs can do, when I get out of the car. Yesterday had a promise, it splashed new and playful, it was carefree, it never learned anything about doubt. There may be a heaviness to today, I don't know, our windows have been rolled up tight all this time.

Better, perhaps, to press on until nightfall. To struggle until night falls. After all, as Cupid despises us most, Night loves us most. She told us so. We have not passed a town in ages, not a single home. This place has forgotten its own name and its own face. Or it was never given one. It was left out here in the cold and the muck, left to speak its name in a slur, in a ramble. It seems to have been forgotten by everyone and everything.

The road continues to lay itself in front of us with distance and no protest. The storm stays ahead, it has nothing to say. Love and I will do it no harm, we don't seek its rain or lighting, we will pass around or beneath. Night begins to awaken, she is wrapping her arms over the storm, soothing it, she cuddles it, and the storm is surrendering. Soon there are some shimmering lights appearing before us. Finally, a place which may have buildings or stores or motels, a name if not a memory.

How quickly the universe can become just we two. The world outside is passive, it gives up its eyes and its ears. I wonder if this is the same night outside as it was inside. There is a different feel to it. I give Love a kiss after a long day in the car, and now there is the melody, now there is the fragrance. There is light within the light. We have a room and a reason to stop.

Night shows her teeth as she smiles, says she is brave enough to wait outside, she winks and offers to gaurd the door.

She is Pleasure's mistress, he gives her a peck on the cheek when she moves aside to let him in. Love and I find ourselves in his jaws, his teeth painlessly clench down upon us, we hang, we dangle here, willingly caught, willingly surrendering, sticking to the roof of his mouth, down, crawling slowly down the darkness of his long warm throat.

Our eyes open in a sigh, there will be no ghosts or sadness tonight, no madness or dreams, no fear or worry. Only sleep, with fronts and backs, faces, and arms and legs. We haven't a clue or care where our clothes might be. They are with the rest of the world, they are hiding out of sight. The road is gone and we have stopped running. The Night will allow us to sleep, she has the gift of making herself longer than the days. Just one last kiss, hovering and longing and reaching, a kiss from soul to soul. And now the devastation of sleep.

=====

There was one cold moment, Cupid tried to poke his laughing face into my mind and then he tried a mask, and I pulled her closer, not giving a thought to what I may have seen.

Day has recovered and rediscovered its grip on the world. Everywhere, including our bed. The moon and the stars left in a panic. I suppose it is time we must move and do something. Love stirs and looks at me with her sleepy eyes. I look back with a promise. We can lay here a little longer. It just gets worse and worse, and she agrees. And until then, and when, and then after and always.

From a hint of color, to amazement to a cloud to a vision, now a flood, a force, a warmth real and in my arms. We could will ourselves not to move today, no to breathe, to stubbornly remain the stillness the world can not move, in a world that refuses to stop. I feel Love moving over me like soft drifting petals. We should stay like this, for all the time that has been stolen from us, for all the time we have been denied. I am lost at her whispering breast, I again have never known this. It is different from the storybooks and the fairytales, it does not drift or float, it comes like a raging waterfall, it drowns the senses until it is the only sense. The last to remain and never fail.

But we rise from this bed finally, standing and feeling the lovepains. I rub my loveworked mouth, stumble a bit on my lovebeaten legs. I ask her if we must drive today, if we must press on. I open the curtains and the windows and the day happily invades with its plans. There is no turning back, no denying it, I look at her with loveworn eyes. I gaze out the window. Nothing looks different, nothing appears out of place. There aren't six black cars, there aren't six angry drivers. Nothing appears to be doing Cupid's bidding. I am thinking about coffee and eggs, as though I am a man without a single worry.

Love says she must look at the map, she does so earnestly, I watch her face. The map is tucked away neatly. We need to go, but not for as long as yesterday. I barely remember yesterday, it is soaked and recovering from my lovememory. We will leave after she showers, this room was but a room and it has no hold upon us. She feels the lovetwists and the loveturns beneath her clothes. She kisses me on the cheek. I feel it all, too, I will just wear them beneath my clothes.

I wait outside, just for the idea of fresh air. It feels like today out here, like a swollen cousin of what we have known. It feels loose and indiscriminate, like we might not be playing by the same rules as we were before. Or someone has changed the game. I turn and face a different direction, and then shift and face another, and then another. Everything feels murky, everything has an oily feel to it. I can't tell which way the wind blows.

I sense some treachery in this day, whether it is real or imagined. Perhaps it is trying to redefine itself. I feel the weight of Cupid's hand upon the back of my neck. I feel his hands like pig's feet, just out of the pickle juice. I suddenly feel we must hurry, we have to run or retreat or vanish. I am alone, waiting beside the car, and I sense I am not alone. I don't know east from west, or here from there, everything is becoming muddied. Love comes outside and we climb into the car. I tell her I am not sure about today, it feels tangled and out of order. Her confidence reassures me. We follow the map and we follow the plan. I know nothing about either. I sit in the quieting warmth of loveblindness.

Love grips my hand. We don't have to go far, we will leave the windows down to leave the scent of blood in the water. Blood for the revenge, blood for the reckoning. We are meandering, leaving a trail. It is not my place to ask why we do not simply disappear. We are tempting fate. We are a noted occurence in the universe, we are a decisive moment. Our shadow trails behind us, our light stretches before us. I ask no questions. My fists feel as though they could face ten Cupids right now.

Today drags its legs behind us, trying to slow us, trying to force us to yield. Love presses harder upon the gas. We are not going home, we are not going to paradise. Not yet. We are going to where we need to be. We are going to when we need to be. I close my eyes, and they awake in the very next moment. The air tastes delicious, I feel Love, soul to soul. And we are going together.

The day has developed a fury, it is no longer following, it is racing ahead of us. Love accelerates and the car lunges forward, but we have lost it around the next bend. I suspect someone has flushed it down the drain. We are traveling slowly again. I wonder if I will be afraid of the truth, when it finally arrives. I wonder if I will be interested. These delicious days with Love, never in my life have I known such days and nights. Days and nights that bring hunger for more. The purity of love, the absence of fear and doubt. We will be pursued until the end, until we find our freedom, and if we can not find it, we will have to create it. Or wait until it is created for us.

We pull into a lot, the car groans to a halt. Evening is waiting for us, it is fat, it has found its way. The sign near the road flickers as though it is trying to wake itself, the letters are turning red. Last Stop Inn. There is nothing remarkable about the place, it seems to cower beside the road as if it is scared of itself. Just another room in a series of rooms, another bed which is not our own. We go inside a the dingey office, I hear the desk clerk shuffling in the other room, a television is on and I hear an old phone drop into its cradle.

His face hangs on him, it is expressionless, it has surrendered many years ago. He simply peddles something that might be close to rest, he peddles it to strangers, an endless line of strangers. A room and a bed, a way to find temporary relief from the highway, a way to get out of the rain. No breakfast, he says, yes, and no promises. If there were such a thing as a bounty on our heads, he has the face of the man who would turn us in. He would sell his friends, his brothers, his own mother, his misery, for the price of a room. But I know there is no bounty. There are no bulletins, there is no police. Cupid wants his revenge, somehow and someway. Cupid wants his revenge in his own way. In his own manner and time.

I don't have to ask how long we will stay here, I know this place and any other place is not on Love's map. I accompany her in an easy blind faith. A faith that is real and has its own flesh and blood, it has its own language and rhythm and song. It is not quite sadness, but there is the smell of old melancholy in the room, not a spark of stinging sadness, just a little wetness, just a little mold. The room's face hangs like that of the desk clerk. Love changes the light, she changes the temperature, she changes the weather in the room.

Love's smile glows against my face, the lovetrance is arriving, the orchestra is stirring. Our souls kiss and tell us we will never know insufferable lovestarvation. The pipes are boiling their water within the walls, the picture turns itself to face the other way, the mirror has closed its eyes. The loveweather in the room is rolling and roaring, the lovetides are rising. Time hushes herself quiet for the moment, the lights are too embarrassed and modest to stay on. The floor is bouncing and the lovemoans are gripping tightly and being suffocated in the lovedance. There is nothing pale and nothing frail, nothing more to hold and nothing to be forgotten. We lay in the quiet loveaftermath.

I realize I am hungry, I am actually starving, as I am finding my clothes. Love is a little tired and she may just rest a while. I offer to bring food here to the room, but she tells me to go, no, Leo, just go. I give her my sweetest kiss, I almost feel a hesitation at the door. If I step out into the dark, will I find the light again. Of course, of course I will. The desk clerk tells me there is a place around the corner, not far from here, it is his brother's place. I walk to it, it is a nondescript diner without much spirit or character but it has something to force into my empty stomach. The cook's expressionless face hangs in front of him, I order from the menu and wait with a can of beer.

My heart is replenished, my legs are loveweak and my mind is loveemptied. I am content for a moment. Perhaps the thoughts of here and there will never return. Love was a destination. I wear her comfortably, her richness, I wear her around my neck and shoulders, she remains in my hands, soft in my hands. Love paints me like a starving canvas. My food arrives and after a couple of hungry bites I feel like I could have another ---

The hot wicked tingles turn to needles and move up my spine. I was convinced I had forgotten them, over these last days with Love. I had abandoned them and they had abandoned me, and now my courage sits next to me like a wet dog. Cupid stands close enough to me to smell him beyond the reach of his cologne. He is right here with my reflection in the glass. He presses one finger into the middle of my sandwich and asks if I am going to finish that. I am somehow frozen, I can not speak, I can not move, I can not flinch or apologize. Cupid is very disappointed, he thought I learned long ago I would never win. And he never loses. I am too cold to shiver, too cold to fear, too cold to panic. One more hand in one last game, Jack, my boy. He is going to show me what it is to lose. He is going to show me what it is to finally lose.

I am paralyzed with Cupid's rancid breath pushing words into my ear. No dice or cards needed for this one, Jack, my boy.

Can't I feel I have already lost? Cupid whispers slow so I can hear every word. I will suffer like no other, I will live the longest, loneliest life, until I beg him for the poison, beg him to end his favorite game. I can feel his teeth at my skin, his rot near my mouth. He says he could end it all right now, he could take my heart like a prize, but he wants it in pieces. And that will take years of misery, Jack, my boy. I unable to think of struggling, I am unable to move, I can't close my eyes. I can't stop listening. Cupid takes half my meal in a bite, my pride in the next, he spits in my drink and laughs.

I have lost the will to speak, lost the will to surrender. I can not fight, I can not struggle. There is only the cold he leaves. He uses a fork to take away the wish that someone might save me. She is a very pretty girl, Jack, my boy. I hope you kissed her before you left.

And with that, Cupid is gone. He was never here. The waitress sees I have stopped eating, I leave a handful of money on the table when she asks if I am doing okay. The world is too quiet. I am hurrying back to our room. Everyone and everything is hiding. I am going to tell Love we should leave tonight, we should not wait until morning. I think they have found us. I do not know what the plan is but we are running out of time. Cupid has his own plan, Cupid has his own intentions. He wants loss and destruction, he is dripping the cherries with chocolate, he wants fear and chaos, he wants to change the game. He only knows how to cheat, he only knows how to ravage and ruin.

I have to tell Love the shadows are coming and the light is getting scared. We can't hide beneath the covers and we can't hide in each other's arms and we can't hide beneath the bed. Cupid is coming and he wants his satisfaction. Cupid is coming and he wants loss and humiliation. He is coming and he will not rest until he has it all in his disgusting filthy hands. I may know nothing of Time and Hope and Temptation, it is Love that I trust. Love will know how to escape, she will lead us out of the darkness and the madness, she will race us back onto the path with the light.

From a short distance, I see there are extra cars parked haphazardly as if they were thrown around the Last Stop Inn. I count them. Six, and Cupid's car makes seven. I walk steadily and purposefully, it is my turn to save her, as she has saved me. It would be easier to flee, easier to run and hide. I will do it forever, if we must, if we have no other choice. I wonder if my hands have any memory, if they have any fight in them.

I am but steps away now, I see a face, a flash of hair through the back window of one of their cars. I feel my legs crumble into the walk of another. I hope he knows how to fight. But now it is my heart, it is mine. I will save her. I haven't an ounce of fear, I haven't an ounce of self preservation left. These strange hands dangling from my arms, they are heavy and light at once.

Cupid's men form a misshapen line in front of me. There is a promise of pain, between me and the car Love is sitting in. I am coming, I search their faces, they have no passion or reason, they don't fear me, they fear Cupid. I have the fearlessness of a man in love, it wraps over me like armor. I have the strength and the need. I have the promise of forever, forever and always.

Another kiss, another helping, another soulful saucy embrace. They stand, waiting for me to move, I stand trembling with true fire coursing in my veins.

This is going to be brutal and heavy and quick, and then

Love and I will race back to the stars, and I will lay with my head in her lap and my hands in her hair. She will drip down upon me, and lavishly drown me. She will bandage both me and this night, she will heal us.

I am suddenly twelve feet tall, I am an army within myself. I feel the steel within my muscles. I love her. We stand, them and I, in the silence that can no longer hold back the moment. I have the courage, I am about to erupt. There will be pain tonight, and then there will be love. I see a hand press against the back window of one of their cars. I stare at each face, I size them up, I feel twenty feet tall. I look into the eyes of all five of them, and realize there were six. I feel a change in the wind, right before the blow rains down upon the back of my head. Cowards. For a moment, I see the ground growing closer.

=====

My eyes return from the bitter blackness and the cold nightmares. I feel nothing but my pounding head, I remember everything. The daylight is falling down upon me, the world looks strange and off balance, as I lay here on my face. The cars are gone and Love is gone and Cupid has won. I am waiting for the screaming to stop, I am waiting for the strength and will to move, to reach our room. I fear the inevitable awaits, I fear my worst thoughts are there. The unbearable emptiness of the room. If I can not stand I can not walk, if I can not walk I can not run, if I can not run I can not chase. My eyes reluctantly close against the pepper of the light. Love must be gone. She has not come to find me.

=====

Whether it is by force or circumstance or intervention, I awake again. I am on the floor of our room at the Last Stop Inn. I look around, carefully, slowly, just beyond the throbbing behind my eyes. The room is not in shambles, it is untouched, it is chillingly still and silent as a secret. I find the strength to roll onto my back, I feel where Cupid's hammer dropped its blow. I have no choice but to lay here. My head feels like wet cake in a bowl. I am waiting for my legs. And then I will find my spirit and determination. I am waiting. And for whatever day it is outside, I do not know you, I do not remember you.

I lay in the drift, I lay in the mud. I am aware of my complaining wounded head, I am aware Love is not here. The weight of the hours pass across my chest, I can not slow them or catch them. My thirst, it is not for water, my hunger is not for food, they are dry in my mouth and gnawing my stomach inside out. It is for her. I am baking in a fever. It was not a love lost or squandered, it was not a love deceived or betrayed, it was not a love mistaken or mistrusted. My love did not fade or erode, it was never distracted, it did not wilt from lack of interest or attention. Love was a gift, love is timeless, and the days were too short. She was taken, she was stolen. My hands were not clumsy, my heart was not clumsy.

I lay restless in this darkening room. Cupid played his final hand in his final game. I should lay here like a snail in this sickening heat, wait for the salt of my own lovetragedy. I groan and find the will to rise and sit on the end of the bed. The crushing weight and strain of the floor is gone. We were together, Love and I, right here, not now but then, our feet were here, our heads were on the pillows. The dismay with the darkness is leaving, it is being scattered, I am slowly feeling my arms and hands, I have shoes again, and feet within the shoes. I knew Love, I know Love, I had her hands upon me. The cold clouds are leaving my mind.

Loss falls from me like tissue paper. My legs have returned and my eyes are new. I could stand like a giant, now, I could stand if I could hear her whisper. A quiet heat is being added to the fever. I can see the Night is pressing fear and pain into the corner, they are trembling, holding each other. Maybe I will hear a knock at the door. Maybe someone will come tell me what day it is. And what I must do next. I start with a shower, to clean my matted head, I throw my shirt into the trash and pull on my last.

With this raw mind I am wading through the thickest hours and waiting for them to thin. In my state, I almost believe I catch a glimpse of her, but no, no, I am alone here in this dark room. The night has nothing more to reveal, I have shaken hands with the agony, I have laughed with the questions that left with no answers. My head will not yet allow a whisper, but my heart can make a promise. I will find her again. I am able to stumble into a slow pace for brief stretches, I will practice until morning.

I had a lifetime without her, followed by days in her arms. This is the cruelty that hangs upon me. I assume hours are passing, judging by the light. The cruelty is losing its sagging weight. I will have my own revenge. The escape is failing like a memory, the plan is the same mystery as it always was. Did Cupid win? I have lost what I had yesterday, if it was indeed just yesterday. I have gained nothing but a wounded head, an emptied room, and a searching heart that was just filled. I am lost among the lost. I can not embrace the solitude again. I am remembering the light on my fingertips, I roll it around, staring at it. I had

Love.

The stink of the morning arrives without much sound or celebration, it arrives without much promise. I had almost drifted toward something resembling sleep. I imagine a loud knock on the door, an explosion of a knock, an intrusive knock. It never occurred to me they might return. I was never in a condition to take on Cupid's men before. My steps are heavy and swollen, and I don't believe my arms have much action in them. I will see this through. The desk clerk with the hanging face is on the other side of the door. He is asking about the blood on the sidewalk, he has noticed our car is gone. He looks around me, says he will be charging for the carpet and the bed, too. He wants me out of the room by ten o'clock. I ask him what day it is. He tells me it is nine o'clock.

I have an hour to collect myself and reassure myself. I am a physical mess, I am an emotional trainwreck. I can be washed off the floors and the windows, I can be forgotten or kept forever. There is a new fresh knocking at the door. It is like a song, it is threatening to blast the door off its hinges. Surely an hour has not passed. I have barely made it to the bathroom and back. I open the door to an unfamiliar face, but she immediately becomes familiar.

It is Time, she looks different away from the shadows, she looks different when she is not moving. I remember her from a dream I once had. She does not ask if I know her, I only nod that I do. I can not speak. She is sorry it had to be this way, it always had to be this way. She is sorry I have suffered.   Cupid had to be coaxed and cornered and baited, he had to believe. His violence had to be awakened, his instincts had to be licked. His animalism and his appetite had to be aroused. His desperate need for loss and heartache was the only way. It could never be simple and subtle, it had to have the lure of devastation and disaster. The richness of human carnage, the deepest despair in the human experience. It was the only way to bring him to the table to feed.

I do not understand at all, but Time smiles and tells me I will. She hands me a book of matches with the logo and name of a pizzeria on its cover. Someone has written Thursday. At 4. And now I have to get all the way back to the city. I have ridden miles and days, and I have no idea where I am. Time laughs. She points and says if I walk to that corner, I turn to the right, and I have to but walk straight. I ask for how long. She says not for long. I don't know where I am going and she tells me I will know what I must do. Time is halfway down the sidewalk when I call out to her and ask her what day it is. It is Tuesday, Leo, it has always been Tuesday.

=====

So perh aps this is the last long and lonely, wandering walk in the journey I never expected and never asked for. The sun insists upon being in my face, whether to cleanse me or prevent me from seeing where I am going. I have become weary of the question of where, of its antagonizing diddling and prodding. I have little more than my thoughts to carry down this path. I have developed a fascination with when, not now or then, but when. That was the plan. When. That was the plan designed for me and disguised from me. When.

If I could whistle or sing to pass the time I would. To remember the richness of the moments, the days and nights spent traveling with my Love. I find myself quickly sinking towards submission and more unanswered questions. My enlightened heart wants to test me, it wants to fail me, the truths I have discovered are trying to fade. I stop walking. I clench my eyes and I can envision her face perfectly, she is frozen in time, she is frozen in my mind. She is taken, and not lost. I walk again as a man who has been pleasured into strength and tricked into weakness. I can feel myself laying in her arms, and my feet are racing to get ahead of themselves.

My steps are growing more steady. I am a man in the world, a world fraught with human nature, littered with the wreckage of distrust and distraction, reeking with the ease of failure, the calm allure of the normal and the common. The cars that pass do not notice me, the people that pass have no faces. I do not want the days I spent with her and the years I wished for to pass like a memory. I want nothing of the carnival, nothing of the hurricane, nothing of life's routines.

I am walking and growing delirious and steady, wanting Love's hips and her lips, her strength and assurance, her calm soothing motivation. I want to be the man I was in her arms. I want to be a better man. My tongue wants to chase her name out into the silence. I want our comfort and our quiet. I want our long meandering truths and daydreams. I want our minutes. I want her eyes searching for mine from the pillow and from beneath her long hair and out in the breeze. I want her healing touches. I want the human taste and the winds of heaven. I want the now and the forever and the simple and the pure. I want the easy devotion, the lightness of discovery and fascination. I want the sensuality and the movements laid bare like a menu upon the sheets in the closeness and privacy. I want the nights, and I want the rosy breath of an angel in the morning.

I want what she gave me, what I never had before. She made her case with style and enchantment, I made no argument and I didn't have to be convinced. I want the familiarity of soulmates. It keeps me from being cold in a place I never wanted to leave.

My mind and legs know what is next. Time spoke the truth, as she always does. It is Tuesday, it has always been Tuesday. I have no desire or need to wander, I might try my best to rest, and do what I know I must do tomorrow. Time's concept of herself, her sense of hours is different from mine, and ours. It is nearly nightfall and I have reached the familiar parts of the city. The familiarity with these streets, the familiarity with solitude. I suppose I could rest beneath a bridge, or sleep in a doorway, or rent a room. Instead, I find myself standing in front of my old place, wondering what the chances might be.

The door is unlocked, I enter and see my pile of possessions and the note I left on top. I crumble the note and pull a chair from the collection. My mind is aching, it is heavy with the confusion of the truth. It has been a long day. I would have never believed there was such a short distance between limbo and heaven. The beers I bought are icy cold and they are going down relentlessly, one after another. I mean to ride them into oblivion, into the soft oblivion beyond the chaos.

Time had no reason to lie, she would have profited nothing from it. So I believe in the clock I have placed back upon the wall. It is beyond midnight, and I drink and pace to no satisfaction. I fall into the hands of Wednesday, it is inviting, it is supposed to be a brief menace. I realize I can not remember the plan, whose it was, and what roles each of us were to play. I do remember Cupid had but one opportunity, one chance, and by the sting in my head, he took it. It is difficult to believe he missed.

One can is freed from my hand and another is captured in its place, I roam from wall to wall, from minute to minute. It certainly feels as though Cupid is winning and I am losing. I have lost the feel of Tuesday, I was there for so long. I can see Love's face and I can not force myself to admit it was all just a dream. I can't accept it. She is my force of nature. My mind struggles to wrap itself around the idea all those lovepossessed nights, they were but a single day. Only my legs and feet move with any freedom. A single thought of Love, it hurts long and dripping and slow along my jawline, it squeezes my neck and my chest. My eyes ache to see her, my ears ache to hear. My heart rages against my ribs, my hands ache to hold, my arms are bewildered.

A loveopera plays in my mind, it duels the silence. I want to ride her like a river, I want her to capture me before I escape. And if isn't fate, there must be a choice, and if not a choice, a chance. A love built for two, beyond the world, beyond the angels' songs, beyond what we know and what we are taught. I must believe in her. My head is gaining ground now, I will soon collapse, and afterwards, I will find tomorrow, it will Wednesday, in some manner of undress.

=====

Love came to me in my dreams, in a wisp, in a cool flame. As soothing as a whisper. And oh how we danced. She is not gone, she is not forgotten, she has not forgotten. Her embrace penetrated me, she wants this soul, my soul. She wants what is hers by right, hers by light, hers by life. With all my might, I tried to give it to her in my dream. We kissed and we remembered. Oh how we kissed. Every place we have ever been, every place we have yet to be. We have a history, she said, and we have a future. We remembered our every touch. As my hands held her tightly and became lost in her long hair, I told her of how I long to relive every moment. My Leo, she whispered, we will not relive them, we will have them. They will be delicate and delicious and new. A peace and a calm and a beauty, we will have what it ours. Our love, never before known, our story, never before told.

Love, on a Wednesday, if only in a dream. I woke without a care for how much of the day was spent and gone. There is hope, layering itself upon me. Let all these hours vanish from sight, let them vanish from memory. These are not the hours I was meant to have, they are not the ones I am meant to keep. This day has no weight and no meaning. There is but one action I must take. I sense no urgency, no worry, there is no panic. This is not my day.

I am comfortable in my clothes today, I am comfortable within my skin. There is but one destination, and it is but a ruse. I walk with an ease I can not remember ever tasting. I stop and admire the flowers, I haven't a care in the world, not in this world, not this today. There is nothing afoot, there is nothing foul, there are no eyes upon me, there are no steps chasing my own. Even the wind moves about as though I am unnoticed. I feel transparent and free. The world may keep itself today, it is not needed here with me. There are no wrong turns today, there is no guide today, today is careening off the rails with no guards or limits.

I am not listless or energetic, I won't struggle and I won't apologize. I am soft and sure and I will not suffer. This is but a dance, this is but a Wednesday trance. I am not at the crossroads, I will seek no bus or train, no plane or boat. I am dust, I am a wet spot on the pavement. I nod politely to humanity, I have no urge to speak or fight. I have no purpose or reason today, I am slick with it, I glide effortlessly with it. I am harmless, I am a man with no past. The Past calls its goblins home, it hurries them like children, it tells them to bring in their toys and shadows with them. It is their bedtime, they do not need me.

Tuesday was enormous, it lasted beyond the counted hours, it hid and drifted, it swelled past its time. And I was scarcely aware. Wednesday hasn't a care of a feel to it, it is in between, it has legs, like it is trying to outrun me. Let it run, I will let it win. I know where the finish line is and it is not here. I will not chase or follow, I will not shout or beg. I don't have to worry about what is in front of me or behind me. I have all the richness of a man destined to be possessed, I'll succumb to it willingly, the sweetness of surrender.

Love on a Wednesday, and oh how we danced.

For the first time, I stand before Cupid's gates without reluctance. His mansion no longer appears forbidding or intimidating. It seems to have shed some of its malice, shed some of its sprawl and its rooms. His men come to meet me, their faces expect a struggle, some act of revenge. I trust blindly in this moment. This is the moment I will see. The men form a familiar line in front of me, this time I count carefully to six. I shrug and show them my empty hands. I believe I am expected, I have no invitation, but I believe Cupid is waiting for me. I can hear him laughing through the windows.

I am escorted inside without a word or incident. There is no reason to fight, the battle is over, the victory has been declared. The victims will simply wash up onto the shore. And Cupid will have his next. I walk into the mansion with all of the weakness and humiliation of the loser. Cupid awaits, fat and smiling like the winner, greasy with the chicken he is eating. I missed the party he threw in my honor, he admits he was a little disappointed. He holds his knuckles near my face. I brace myself, there is a new ring on one of his fingers, a ring he stole from some lover out there somewhere.

His breath is hot and cynical, he wants to tell me a tragic story. My story. His hand reaches into a bowl of cake, he brings a fistful to his greedy mouth. Some makes it to his teeth, some falls onto his neck. He squeezes it out the rest between his fingers, just like he has his hands in my guts. I always win, Jack, my boy, and everyone else loses, especially you. The ugly truth to Cupid's games, that each one is his favorite, each one is his own, each one is decided before it begins. If you are playing you have already lost. My eyes burn and tell themselves not to worry, they are willing themselves to blink. I try to keep my heart cold and broken. I used to be afraid here. But not today.

Cupid farts loudly and belches, he says he has lost his taste for me. And when the dice and the cards are still, when the darts stop flying, that is the end, Jack, my boy. I am the first one he has ever stopped playing with. He says he was a little surprised when I stole his car, and he is certain it was not my idea. I never held that kind of hand. His smile is full of spit and despair, cake and nausea and chicken. And wounded souls. I stand with a surprising strength, I should have wilted or cowered by now. He has grown tired of me, he has become bored with my suffering. His smile turns green and wicked. He sits heavily into his chair. One of his bunnies hurries over with a cigar and lights it. I stand here, trying to be small. He waves his fat hands around to empty the room. He offers me one last parting game. I shake my head, we have already played his last game. Cupid strokes his belly in amusement, and wasn't it just a gas, Jack, my boy. He tells me he is going to exile me like a prince. To suffer in silence the rest of my years, for the rest of eternity. He is going to abandon me to the darkness. But first!

I am a trophy mounted on Cupid's wall. I recognize my own stark face. He shows me how he has put a new spotlight on it. See how there was almost some will in your eyes, Jack, my boy. This is his final parting shot, consider it his hug goodbye. He has a new trophy and he wants me to see it. He insists I see it, he insists I take a moment to admire it. He is most proud of this new one. He tells me I should have come to the party, I should have been obedient, my life could have remained an easy wreck. Cupid grinds out his cigar. Don't worry, Jack, my boy, she will be exiled, too, in time. A prince and a princess in exile, never to have, never to be.

I am a trophy mounted on Cupid's wall, it is where I have always been. I am still the most famous, I am still anonymous. He despises me most. He despises us most. I win again, I always win, he says, and his laughter grows. Anyone and everyone can be Cupid's prize. Life goes on, squished within his hands. He will give me a minute. Sixty seconds, sixty heartbeats, as a favor I never asked for. Then I will be escorted to the door, banished for all time. He nods for the cover over his new trophy to be removed.

I stand in silence, for the full sixty seconds, counting them as they fall across my shoulders. I pretend to suffer his joyous look. It is remarkable, the physical similarities between

Love and Temptation. They could not have been twins, but sisters, for certain. There is a different look, a different feel, around their eyes and mouths. A different heat, a different purity. Temptation appears to wink at me, telling me not to worry, she is fine, she can not be captured, she can not be contained. It is time to leave, I want to tell Cupid I will see him, I will see him on the other side. There is no other side, Jack, my boy, I have taken it all from you, there is nothing left. The door closes behind me. I look up and breathe, I feel freedom on my face.

=====

I am holding my own, maintaining my personal space and private thoughts in the drift. Wednesday seems to be teetering and drunk now, uncertain where to land and how to end. I wish I had a way to help it. I am no where in particular to be now. Night is coming, She is dropping her colors all around. I walk past rows and rows of glass houses with opened windows, I haven't the slightest concern or curiosity of what may be going on inside. The city, and everyone alive within its arms, they are building themselves, bracing themselves for an evening, for everything it may offer, for everything it may forget. No one seems to notice where I am walking. This must be the feel of exile, prince or not. I will take the detours if there are no roadblocks, I will take the long way around. I hope the hours forget some of their minutes. I hope Wednesday pulls itself together, gathers its clothes, and goes to sleep. I hope Time remembers this was all her idea, I hope She does become distracted or bored. I have played my small role. I have grown so tired of waiting, I have been waiting my entire life.

No matter how we might struggle and strain, we, none of us, can force the action. We may control what we see, what we hear, what we purchase, we may rule what we own, we can turn on the lights and turn on the music. Desire can be pursued, but passion has hands of its own, they can not be coerced or begged, they will not be hurried, they will act as they will. So I am walking, not chasing, walking, not searching. I am certain I will eventually find my way back to my place, but not yet. The nights last too long there.

Time will not change reality for one little man. The world must continue to spin and grind, it will never alter its dizzying dance. I try to relax, I try not to complain, but Wednesday seems to be trying to prove it can be the longest. It no longer wants to run the fastest or jump the highest. It is trying to be the laziest of days. I would offer it a bus ticket, a free tropical vacation, whatever it may take. If I get hungry I could eat, that may help a little, maybe if the cook has a bad finger, or the waitress has tired legs.

Here in the thick mud of evening, there is no way around it and no way through it, I won't consider retreat having come this far. The food here did smell delicious, and I wait, staring at a wall of silent televisions. I am curious without worry, how tomorrow might taste. I hope to be able to tell the difference, to name the difference, between it and now and today. I know Night will make her prompt exit. Perhaps the sky will be the same color, the dance will maintain its rhythm, fire will reclaim its heat. There is always the hope the hours will lose their steady path and their place and their restraint. I eat in the noise and slowly realize the noise is from the room filling with strangers. We are strangers touching only with our voices and our shoulders. It is like a crazy trapeze act, not making eye contact or conversation. I stay for a couple more drinks to heavy this mind of mine, to take another bite out of this evening. Once I am back outside, I breathe the good air, free from the congestion, away from the activity. I do not want to be a beggar, I do not want to be annoying. The drinks will help with the weight of the wait. I realize I am not deprived, I am unburdened by the details of Time's idea and Hope's plan. I can only assume the goal was a reunion, or at least discovery, a fleeting moment, a whispering chance.

I believe I can make out the best part of the night's sky overhead. I wonder if Love sees it and sees it as I do. I do not where she is. I know Cupid does not possess her, as he believes, and she is not here in my arms. I am in exile and she may be anywhere. But I must believe she is close, not just beyond my hands or just around the corner, she is close. It is a sudden comfort, I relax my will and my worry, I offer neither resistance or struggle. This drift is not time, it belongs to Time, I allow myself first to float, and then be carried. I may as well close my eyes.

I am back at my old place, I leave the world outside the door. It is not mine, I don't belong with it tonight, I have no need for it. I will drink greedily in hopes I will sleep greedily, and soft with dreams. Night patiently stokes the embers of her fires, the flames are rising the deepest richest blue before they will turn to black. She tells me not to worry, she has the world for just a few more hours, she never stays longer than she should. Wednesday is teetering on that dull edge as if it is afraid the air and the space beneath won't catch it. Wednesday makes a face as though it is about to throw a tantrum. Night knocks loudly upon my window,

I open it and let her in. She is dressed like a mother, she has come to gather the children and make them hush and brush and go to bed. Wednesday is first, it is time for sleep, it's turn will come again.

And then Fate with its bag of mischief, then Sadness with its weight, and finally Fear with its nervousness. They are all placed in bed with the covers pulled warm and tight to their chins. Shh.... shh... tomorrow is already coming. I don't know if she is talking to me or them. As I am closing the window behind her, Night offers me one comfort as she turns to leave. I should check my pockets for anything from the past, I won't be in need of them tomorrow. I have nothing but a pack of matches, I toss them onto the counter. I may be the only man awake right now, I wait and do not chase the hour at which I could find myself stretched, finally, resting finally, on a bed built for one, possibly meant for one. But it could be stretched or shrunk to hold two. Two in the quiet, two in the night. I lay on my side, searching the place Love would be, I try to find her in the darkness. There is no face there, there are no eyes, no smile or laughter. Not tonight. I wring my hands free of worry, and now comes the slow submission into sleep. Night said tomorrow is already coming, it is nearly here.

=====

The wild carnival ride of sleep, I am led, I am ridden, I am sped down the trails, whipped at the haunches, spurred at my sides. I blast past the fortresses and the castles. I have no business within, I have no seat at the tables, I have no stake in the treasures. My sweat is in my nose, there is foam in my mouth and at my lips. The lights are a blur and the joyous laughter slips past like stolen minutes. I am careening towards the cliffs, the dust is in my eyes but I can see them coming, and I am wondering who is riding and who is in charge. I am pulled hard right, and then to the left. The finish is no where in sight.

Again, again. They want nickels for the ride, dimes to rest, quarters for dreams, dollars for peace. To their amusement, I find myself saddled and empty handed.

But now I can see sleep in soft layers, sleep in a lazy river, sleep in a comfortable enveloping fog. Sleep falls upon me in chunks, in boulders, I am run through cactus fields. It is just another element that has its hands on me, has its turn with me. My eyes are half opened, they are half closed, I see the colossus rise from deep within the ground and step over the mountain and wade into the sea. It seems to be complaining about me. It prefers the day. I have never asked anything from it, it is but an interruption. It wreaks havoc and speaks no words I have ever known.

I never trusted Sleep or what he hides behind the curtains. He has always been searching for someone else. And now he tosses me and turns me, sears me on all sides. I can't fit into his cradle, I can't fit into his arms. Sleep is too harsh, too immediate, too brutal. He won't make me deaf, we won't make me blind. As enormous as he is, he can not crush yesterday, he can fulfill no promises tomorrow. Sleep drips slowly upon my forehead, as though bored, as though telling me he would rather not be here. Not with me, he doesn't care for my shy and loud and refusals. He could spread himself elsewhere in the universe, serve as an escape, a balm for a wound. He could be out there pretending to be a luxury, or dressed as forgetfulness, or forgiveness, or stalking the lazy. Whether in the shadows or the light, Sleep has these same eyes, peering at me, asking if I want to. Sleep has its own memories and demands.

I hope Sleep can peel away the hours of this day, I hope he can cut its legs short. He can have the hours, keep them, or throw them out the window into the streets. Whatever brings me closer, whatever brings me out of the cold and back to Love. I writhe beneath the steady pressing weight, my bones have not asked for it, my soul asks for the light and movement. My mouth aches for tomorrow. Sleep speaks to me with a slow drawl and a stutter. I understand, everyone understands. I will have cotton in my eyes, whiskers on my face, I want wings on my back, so I will find tomorrow.

I finally succumb and am falling into the sweet distance. There is a light. These are the true elements within the universe, the energies and forces which maintain and guide us through the universe. They all have their wet grip on the human experience. I can name them all, I have been touched by them all. They gather like kings and queens, but I will not serve them. Their names and their promises, I can count them all across my fingertips, as though I were counting sheep. I would rather surrender to but one.

There is Cupid, there is Time. There are Hope and Night, Temptation and Fate, Sleep and Fear, Justice and Sadness, Memory and Mood, Passion and Forgiveness, Dreams and Lies, Compassion and Promises, Destiny and Truth. They sit in a circle because none is above the other. They fight at times, sometimes they join hands, but none reveres another. These are the elements of the universe. Some may pokes us, some may feed us, bury us or lift us or fear us.

And then there is Love.

=====

I wake this morning with sleep on my face, it is tight and sloppy, it is reluctant to leave, reluctant to let go. I have it in my elbows and my knees and the small of my back. I simply want to get on with the day. Today. I look different to myself in the mirror. There is a spark and a charge, life pools around my eyes. My hands and legs feel as though they are eager for a purpose, a destination. An end to the silence and the wandering.

I am not a trophy on any wall. I am an empty slate, I am a hungry wishing well, I have a heart that wishes to flower. I want to take root. There is something about the mood and movement of this day, it is fluid, it is beckoning from outside the windows. I have faith in this day, it is solid in my chest. There are two possibles, I will take them over the one hundred impossibles. Yes, yes, I am coming, yes, I have eaten and my pants are on. Everything seems quite right. I am being thrown towards life and my eyes are opened.

There is a flavor in the air I have never tasted. I will count the minutes as a man who will soon have no memory, I will selfishly count them as a man who will soon have memories. My own steps seem to take two to my one. Something is calling to me, something is calling. I am not lost, I am not falling, I am not swaying or dangling. There is something missing which must be found, something searched for which must be true. I am alive in the sweet honey and the sweeter light. There is the sense the ending will dwarf the beginning in heat and length and magnitude. The ending will be the fruit and the oil, the ending will be all I need. The beginning is what my fingers and teeth are reaching for. The beginning is what must be right.

I walk a road I have never traveled, I live a day I have never lived. Peace and fascination are growing closer, it is comforting, having them stalking me. They may grow fond of each other. They may grow fond of me. There is no restlessness, no wandering, no crush of wonder. Not today. I have no need for confidence or worldly instructions. My role is within the when. I know when. I have been told when. There is no mischief to this day. The people and the animals and the creatures are all in their places. It is too bright to see if the stars are aligning into a smile, it is not time for them to show their faces. I feel like I am walking freely in a long line of souls, it is the first chance I have ever had. This is my first ride and my last ride. I am in the comfortable line of souls, none of us look back, or left or right. Some are waiting to erupt, some are waiting to reunite, some are simply passing through.

This is my exit, my last corner to turn, my last step to be taken while in no possession of a past. There is only today and tonight, and the push beyond the manmade feelings of luck and lust. I am drawing ever closer, somewhere between clarity and forgiveness, between cleansing and rebirth. It will soon be decided. Who has the courage and who is the coward. There are only two pieces in this moving day. My soul is free and open, my heart is starving. I have only one question. Will she be there?

I arrive before it is time, I am raw and new and early, I await the moment Time herself has orchestrated. I had the courage to come, I have the courage to be patient. Time has scorched a line across the ground. It is not a challenge, it is the finish. It is the beginning. I am here, ready for all the possibilities, ready to have nothing and everything. I have nothing more to see, I have nowhere else to be. I am here, with want and hope.

It is the world that is the coward. It seems stunned, maybe even insulted to have none of my attention. It attempts to gather everything and everyone, for there is safety in numbers, and it knows it. Four o'clock is looming, it is spilling over the dams and spilling around the edges, four o'clock is peering through the fences. This slow parade is the last chance the world has left to pull from its bag of party tricks. I can read it upon all these unknown faces. The world is terrified, it does not want to lose the comfort of the common. The past wants to be justified, the future wants to be predictable, the present wants to remain an icebath. The parade becomes louder and thicker and more manic. I feel only this fever, the hour is approaching, it is ringing the bells. The world is the coward, terrified everything is about to change. There is a lovemystery, a lovestory, the blood is boiling into ink. And nothing will ever be the same again. It is a lovestory to be written over history and reason, a humble lovestory to take but a small corner. It is time, it is time. The parade grows silent, just a wash of faces. I close my eyes and whisper some reassurance to the world as it tips on its axis. We will be gentle, we will be kind, even as it was cruel. Love is gentle.

The parade and I, you, and me, everything, we are beneath the heavy landing, the moment's crushing arrival. I do not struggle to swim or struggle to survive, I breathlessly wait for the moment, for the familiarity, for the memory to appear in the light. I am ready. The air returns to fill the void and soon the oxygen does, too. The minutes have restarted and they work to smooth out the wrinkles.

The parade restarts with new movements and unrecognizable faces. I sense cautious footsteps approaching. I feel them grow louder, shedding caution for beautiful confidence. This is our day, this is our time. Time and Hope and Temptation all have color in their cheeks, they are blushing, they are gushing. A woman appears from the thick mist of the parade. I have never seen her before, not in life, not in a dream. She removes her sunglasses and her eyes whisper, my Leo.

=====

I am loveentranced, I aware of your first words, and now they flow over me like milk, they are soothing, they are an invitation. Your words speak beneath themselves, you ask how I am doing, I hear you, I hear when you say oh there you are. You begin in the middle of a conversation we had lost ages and lifetimes ago. My eyes search around your voice to find your mouth. It will take but a moment for it to be perfectly kissed. You laugh and I search around it for your eyes, they whisper to me, I run to them like home. We are loveshadows, you and I, tantalizingly close to where we need to be.

This lovesickness, the fever within the truth, denied and distorted, hidden and concealed from us. We can not stand with it, we can not sit with it. We are forced to walk, and walk happily with it, until our steps learn their dances, until the dances reach their purpose. We walk into the evening, the world is out here again, realizing we mean it no harm. We walk with my hand dangerously close to yours, we walk and spill memories and stories, they fall from us like snowflakes, they fall from us like burdens, like crunching sacks of stones. There are only footsteps behind us, there are no pasts. We talk long into the evening until She threatens to give up. We walk towards our first memory, our first lovememory to be. We have found our names and our faces, our shelters, our dreams shared of promises yet to be. Time smiles down upon us, she is quietly removing her talents, we don't need her hands or eyes any longer. She allows Never and Before to fade into the distance, they disappear among the relics. There is only Forever and Always. And Now. Night has dressed herself in layers, she is eager to wait, eager to allow us these harmless freedoms. Our hands remain treacherously close, nearly brushing against one another. I will want to kiss you tomorrow.

This is the last narrow path we will walk. I don't want any of the steps I have taken, I don't want any of the steps you have taken. Our souls have already disrobed, the Past clutches its own empty arms and realizes it can not follow. We press the hours in front of us, I can see clearly through the fascination, I can hear and feel clearly through the newness. I am warm through the loveshivers. We have a steaming writhing history, you and I, one that has suffered in a box, in silence. A history never to be denied again, a history to be briefly remembered, with a future crashing fast upon us. The language you speak is the same as my own, the same accent and strange dialect. Our melodic lovetongues rarely used and never forgotten. Neither of us have a plan, we have no idea where we are going, we are nearly out of the reach of the last of the eyes. We are lovelost and lovefound. You smile, you are comfortable with me, you are at ease for the first time in your life, we will go deeper there, into this night, for as far as this night allows. The Night opens her arms wide, we can go as far as we would like.

We are here between what is known and what is to be

held, what is unknown and what is to be cherished. We are beyond the thorns and filth and tar of chance, and approaching sweet and lush discovery. I whisper to you through your hair, tell me everything you want me to know.

Just before we escape the last of the city's lights, I pass a familiar image, he is trapped behind a window. Cupid stares at us with his muted rage and jealousy, he watches powerlessly as we walk past. He has never seen us together, you and I. And he will never see us apart. He has no voice and no arrows, he has no tricks and no games for us tonight, or any other night. He has the look of a boy no one wants to play with. He will never be in my dreams again, he will never invade my choices, he will never ruin my chances again. We are not trophies on his wall. You are Love, and I am your Leo.

We find each other in the darkness, we are just within reach of surrender. Your eyes search into mine, I allow you to see everything you wish to see. My hands nearly take yours, there is a hold that is coming, it is as inevitable as tomorrow. Oh, if you will agree to tomorrow, and your sultry walk and sultry talk tells me you will. You have collapsed my walls and my soul is playing like a child in your fingers. We have blossomed from strangers to lovesurrender and this night still continues to whisper around us. I don't want to count the hours. I want to know what I have never known, I want to taste what you can show me. I don't need to know where you are taking me, I want you to know that is where I must be. Their faces and their words and their hands can not find us now, not here where you keep me, and I keep you.

I hesitate like a gentleman, and you allow me to, like a lady. I respectfully pause, and you respectfully decline. There is no hurry to this lovedance. We are not of this age, we are not in the trappings, not in the fishnets or the televisions. It is your soul and your heart and your mind I want. These six hours we have kept to ourselves look sickly and ravaged, but they can be nursed back to health, they can be resurrected. I ask for but a couple more, innocent and true, without bravado, this urge is patient like a fever. I will have my hands soft at your face, my kiss upon your lips, my eyes buried within yours. In time. I ask humbly for this woken dream to last a little longer. I haven't the steps, I haven't the hips, I am up for the challenge, I am ready to learn. There is nothing in the world which glows like you tonight. I am loveenraptured, I am lovecaptured, my longing hands are in my pockets. I have learned to smile tonight, it will take longer to dance without clumsily reaching, without stumbling. I do not want my anxious hands to muddy the spiderwebs or muddy the songs. There is a perfect picture and a perfect moment standing right before me now.

We are loveshadows, growing so close to where we have been meant to be. These last dribbles and drops of tonight, they peer at our faces, they follow our words and our steps, and we don't mind. They are wondering what we will do. We are true and unmasked, we are smiling and neither of us can break the spell. I will kiss you tomorrow. Your kiss is waiting for you tomorrow. The world can watch from its balconies and its clouds. I will ache new tonight, I will ache new in the morning. Our souls know they have ridden the long lonely trains, through the darkest meatless years. We are here, we are here now. Never to regret, never to forget, without a hint of sorrow. It is amazing how quickly your charms and magic have begun to work. Give me one more smile.

Between the first breath and the final eclipse of a single evening, I have become. I am transformed. We have become. I hear it in our voices, I see it in the way I am starving for you and you are relieved I have not lunged at you once, we have maintained a soft distorted distance, a roaming, swirling reunion. The world has regained its strength and color, it is colored like a garden of our roses. This is not the pale love, the parlor love. I may be done with yesterday, I long for tomorrow. What will you bring me? I want a dream I am possessed by, and here you are, standing three feet away. I see there are soft pools in the sky, I invite them to fall like rain. We don't need the dirt from the roads we have traveled, we don't need their dust or their given names. We don't need the words and opinions, the doubts and the rejections. They can't follow us anymore. They do not fit here, there is no room. We are lovestruck, we are lovethrown and lovedrunk.

If you will not forget me tonight, you never will.

I will not sleep tonight, I haven't the legs for it, I have too much within me. I wonder if you can still see me smiling, I wonder if you can still hear it in my voice. I needed you for lifetimes, we deserved each other for lifetimes. I am too swollen with this one night to allow it to rest. Tonight was given to us, gifted to us, we were destined for it, it was carefully planned. It was in our hands. I don't want to dream another dream, I don't want to wait another minute. I kept my arms from you, I kept my hands from you, I kept my desire from you. I am in a place larger than a world I have ever known. We will wait one day. I secretly, desperately, want to come find you again. I want to love you as no woman has ever been loved, and that will make me the happiest man who has ever lived. I will drown my thoughts and tell them to just be proud of themselves in their silence. My feelings are another beast, they are one I can not tackle and maintain.

I can not unsee your face. I can only hear your voice tonight. My Love, everything I said to you was true, tonight. Everything I will say, will be true. I hope you are waiting for tomorrow, I hope you are waiting for me. I hope you are warm in your bed and making room for me, the covers may not fit me, the room may be to small, but I find my heart is here and with you and it is not leaving. I will not forget you tonight, and I never will.

I awake alone against my pillow and wonder if it will be for the last time. My list of lovedemands is short. I want to see you again today. And I will, after the delays and the detours and the obligations. I notice a single long strand of your hair has made it into my bed. I stare at it, not wanting it to move. I need the rest of you here now. I can lay heavy in this lovetrance for a while, I don't want to sit and count the hours. The world can fill with hate and lies, with soup and mustard, with flies and honey, I will not be pried from this day. Yesterday was but the beginning of this song. I hum a little and smile to no one but myself.

I have another chance, at the first chance. Minutes with you stretched long into hours, hours into redemption. Redemption into dreams. My face was cracked with a grin, my eyes were hungry, I was not nervous for one moment. You were not afraid, you were mostly amused. You said we could meet again today, that today was not too soon, there are no games to play, there are no roles to play. There is no pace to maintain, no etiquette to upset. I didn't want to scare you, so I didn't even whisper it, I didn't think it too loudly. You said you are scared of nothing. I have loved you since we created fire, I have loved you since men first sailed the deepest blue, I have loved you since man took flight and cars were invented, I have loved you through war and peace. Our stolen lives and misplaced centuries, this is our chance. The chatter and the lies, the mischief, it can all be forgotten. The weight of the waiting has left us. We are abandoned and free. Your past has run screaming, terrified and lost in the darkness, and so has mine. I need but one inviting glance.

I want to be in the grip of you and all your sultry things. I want the story to hurry past the beginning. I will risk everything. I want to love you with bare hands, I want to love with the hunger of souls, once the hearts and minds have taken to their nest. I have sensed your power and your perfection, I will be patient as I watch them evolve. I am thirsty, to have met you once is not enough. Tell me your dreams and give me more reasons to stay. Bring them to my ears and my eyes, leave them at my lips or pour them onto my tongue.

There are no lovetransgressions, there will be no lovesins. Not at the heights we will reach. I noticed your wings on the other side of your shirt, bring me into your wake, I am here to let you fly. If I am to have you, you must be unchained and unleashed. We will start somewhere beyond the reason, start beyond the clouds. We can start where the light has not dared to look and our whispers can not be found. My mind is gorged with lovecandy, I wonder where your thoughts are today. I need you to breathe air into this room. I have the lovesnaps and the lovejitters, I am trying to feel my feet at the bottoms of my legs. This isn't the angry or lost pacing I have always known, this is the patient, anticipating pacing. I am marking off the minutes and the hours, I am spending them like nickels and dimes. I will be happily lovecrushed beneath these rolling stones. The morning has made a fool of itself, forgetting half of itself, I am already shaking hands with the afternoon.

I don't know where you are, but I don't have to find you anymore. You have whispered the weather into my ear, these are going to be better days. I can picture you in a place, in a moment, and you are lovely, you look like my favorite. The lovesplash is nibbling away, the day is beginning to feel it, it is beginning to understand. It is considering collecting itself, making way for the exiled, making room for the lovers. Us and all the rest. We are an anxious growing mob. The day is going to step aside, maybe get a wash, go to the tailor for a custom suit for a special occasion.

My door opens to the hungry world outside, I am hungry, the streets are hungry for the traffic, the sidewalk is hungry for my steps, passing faces are hungry, the moon is hungry for the sun, everyone and everything, suddenly hungry. Nothing has been satisfied for too long. Nothing has been right. Nothing has been fair. I have hungry hands for this evening, I have hungry wishes. You have given me your address, my hands have stopped trembling with it. When you told me, it sounded like you said, shh, I trust you. I arrive in time to smell the moon has cooled to blue and the stars have been set. I reach just beyond the touch of your hand. Perhaps just beyond this lovemadness we can find a dinner. In a crowded room, we are the only two, just above the storm, we are the only two. We are sitting across from each other, I will never forget your face. Love scribbles its way across the top of the table, I can see and hear every word. I don't know how soon is too soon, I don't know how right is too right. I keep my hands on my dishes and my fork and knife, and my heart is spilling from my shirt. You see it and smile in every direction.

The room has become loose and alive, I am wanting to bury ourselves out in the night, somewhere. I want the hours to show mercy and slowly bend. You are as close as a breath beside me, and just out of reach. I need but an invitation, your eyes tell me I have but to ask. Or not ask at all. We have finally lost all the paths we have known. I feel it in our steps, I feel it in our easy steps. There is no pain or forgiveness in the air tonight. We are new, we are reborn. I have loved 100 times, and I know I have only loved you. And your eyes burn into me, asking how long you will have to wait. Two more corners and a twist and a plea to the Night to not bed herself so soon.

Night goes soft between us and slowly moves out of the way. The stars return to their villages in their forests. The only light is upon our lips. Our hands ache with old want. We are standing in front of your place, safely in the shadows, just within reach of the lurking eyes. You will teach me to dance, one day, you have taught me to believe. Something has taught me how to kiss your mouth perfectly. We have lovehands, shaking the cookie jars. It is sometime before midnight, it might be time for the neighbors to leave their windows and return to their televisions.

You speak with a lovebreath, in a tone somewhere between encouragement and satisfaction, slightly past decency and closer to invitation. We were born for this and made for this. The universe will never be the same, but we have endured its best and its worst, this is our chance and our moment. We look at each other with honeymoon eyes, drifting so close into a second night's kiss. A first kiss. I linger and hover, long and longer. The universe will forget its name, with this nameless kiss, this lovesoaked kiss, this kiss we have endured all of our lives to taste. The moment is alive within me, just beneath your hands, your eyes are waiting. You are lovely in this moment, in this movement, you are mine. Our kiss is a loveflash, and the lovesecrets nearly knock us to the ground, we hold each other close, we survive.

Your fingers spread lovespeak across my face. My eyes find yours, we are the only two alive. Drenched and lovewilling, lovefound. It took but one long centuries' awaited kiss. To become alive I will drown in you, I will sleep within your wings. I will be your truth if you will be mine. I will be your shoulder, I will give you as many smiles and every smile you need. I will be the back that can bear, the arms that can hold, the hands wild with want. I will be your partner as we conquer, I will be your partner if we only make it, barely, dangerously, driftingly close, I will be the dreamer you can confess to, the best friend to reveal secrets to, I will be your pleasure and your lover true. And you will be mine.

I will find the words, one day, my Love. I will find where they fly. I am a gentleman and not a coward, a lover and not a thief. You have a pleasure and softness and daring strength that will bring me to the edges. Bring me wherever you wish, we will never demand or follow. We are in step, now, a beautiful step, side by side. I am yours and you are mine. We don't have to explain or acknowledge the suddenness, the glorious recklessness of how we have come to be. I will always find your heart, where it is soaring and free.

We will part, if but for hours, and the noise and the lights will not follow us.   This moment was ours. You wrap it around my shoulders so I can carry it with me, I can feel it. I will remember it, turn my face into it, feel it drip down my neck. Your steps begin the reluctant shuffle towards your door. I could stand out here all night. But the meat is in the dish, waiting for the sauce, waiting for the heat, tomorrow has the heat, and tomorrow has the answer, tomorrow in an endless line of tomorrows. I realize only these legs could have made this journey, from the never had to the then to the dreams to the now. Your eyes are telling me you are falling in love, your eyes are telling me this is not goodbye. You whisper, if we can, my Leo, if we might.

And now, the warmth and the wonderment, I step out of the light and into the light. I walked through your door and never left. You had to have me as I was. I am home, this is home, you are home. We are here and everything else remains outside. The need for comfort ceases, comfort simply exists. These walls are ones I feel I have known before, I touch them and call them by name, they are familiar and inviting. I follow you out into your gardens, I will follow you anywhere. Yes, the past with its long harrowed face shrugs and turns away. The future is somewhere to be made, perhaps beneath the roses. It is hiding within your words. Your hands drift warm into mine. The world patiently waits beyond, it allows us our peace.

There is an understanding here, with you and I, there is a dream, there are a thousand dreams. I have drifted so far from the gray, now there are only the tones of love. Nothing is coming to find us in the darkness, nothing is searching for us in the silence. It is you and I, my Love, in this home you found, in this home we are making. Creation begins with but a breath, it begins with a trust. The rest falls into lines, it falls into balance. My straight lines, and your curved lines.

I watch as your sundress floats in the sunlight, your steps press sweetly into the earth. Your magical dance. I smile, thinking of you wearing the wedding dress of my wife one day. I am lovedevoured, I have lovesurrendered. We relax in the afternoon, I close my eyes, wishing you would consume me faster. But I relish your slow teeth and your slow throat, I relish your heart and your soul. I have no where else to be, but in your hands. I breathe, so take your time. I am here, we are here, and we will never leave.

Ours is a love never to be escaped, never to be betrayed. It climbs over the walls, it climbs over the mountains, it hangs pretty in the moonlight, it hangs thick through the years. There is just us. You can be my wife, my best friend, my temptress, my soulmate. I can be me, and anything you need. I will offer only everything that I am, all that I have, anything I might evolve into. The afternoon dances away from us, and we offer no pursuit. I just want a kiss.

I know when the muses were created, when the mothers had them all swaddled and safe, when the muses were infants and innocent, that is when they chose you to be mine. I have found the will to begin our story, your story. My Love, and all your sultry things.

About the Author

Born in Michigan in 1974, the narrator has spent the majority of his life in various regions of North Carolina. He happily, peacefully resides with his wife in Sneads Ferry. He works full time hours in the trenches at the butcher's shop, he writes in his garage. In the quieter moments, he enjoys expanding the flower gardens with his wife, and spending time with their six children and grandson.

Made in the USA
Monee, IL
04 July 2024